# OUR Totally, Ridiculous, Made-Up CHRISTMAS RELATIONSHIP

Brittainy C. Cherry

Our Totally, Ridiculous, Made-Up Christmas Relationship



Edited By: Mickey Reed

Cover Design By: Berto's Design

Interior Design By: Jovana Shirley, Unforeseen Editing



ISBN-10: 1494447827

ISBN-13: 978-1494447823

# Dedication

*To the hopefuls who believe in the magic of ridiculous, silly, and playful love.*

*Keep Dreaming. Keep Believing. Keep Loving.*

*XoXo*

# Contents

# Acknowledgments

I would like to start by thanking YOU, the person who is reading this. For so long these stories have lived in my head and I never dreamed that one day people would be taking this journey with me and giving my words a chance. Giving *me* a chance. It means the world to me that you took the time out of your lives to read my work, and I hope you received a bit of enjoyment from the experience. XoXo

To my fellow authors—only you can truly understand the fears, the joy and complete madness of this world we live in. I have come across so much talent in this year alone that inspires me to hone my craft. Thank you. Keep writing and I'll keep reading.

My beta team—the best team ever. Thanks for ripping my novels apart just so I can put them back together, better than ever.

A shout out to Abby's Book Blog—for all the help you gave me for this novella!

To my Dream Team: Rebecca Berto at Berto's Designs for the amazing cover. Mickey at I'm A Book Shark, the amazing editor that she is. Debbie Popp Haumesser, thank you for your proofreading skills. I love you so, so much! Jovana at Unforeseen Editing—thanks for your awesome formatting skills! I love you all!

To my best friends—too many to name, yet all so important. Thanks for loving me even though I go MIA while writing.

To the siblings Bryon, Tiffani, Brandon, Candace, Isaiah, Ben, Will: So much love, respect, and pride to be able to call you all family. Love you!

To my papa: Thanks for the love and support! Love you, dad!

Lastly, this one is for you, mom: The one who believed in my dreams when I didn't know how to. Thank you for standing me in front of the mirror at a young age and having me say over and over again, "I am somebody. And I have a voice." You're the Sherlock to my Watson. Love you to the moon and back!

# 1 Kayden

## Home for the Holidays

A family gathering. That's the last way I want to spend my Wednesday night. Why the hell do people act like they actually enjoy these get-togethers, when secretly, they all hate each other's guts? I mean, let's be real. You wouldn't hang out with those people if they didn't have your last name, right? This sucks ass.

Pulling up to my parents' house, I toss my cig into the car's ash tray, cussing under my breath at how annoyed I am with myself for buying another pack. Yesterday I was supposed to have my final smoke, but then Dad called irritating the living hell out of me.

My hands travel through my hair, and I glance in the rearview mirror, rubbing my fingers over my tired eyes. No sleep last night—my full attention was on Britney. Britney…or was it Whitney? The palm of my hand flies up to my eyes and I squint, trying to grasp the faded words and numbers. Eva. How the hell did I get Britney from Eva? Oh well, it doesn't matter.

My tongue runs across my hand, erasing the lasting ink stain from existence. Never gonna call her again. She might still show up at Hank's where she met me, cocktail wizard that I am behind the bar. It's a known fact that girls flirt with bartenders, and I've made more than my fair share of trips back to random apartments, always with a different chick on my arm. That's where Britney—er—Eva met me. That's where all of the girls meet me. I never led her or any of them on, and I am very straightforward with each girl, telling them that it was only sex and nothing more. That way, I'm pretty sure if any of them build up some fairytale romance then it's on them, not me.

I look toward the enormous home before me and slowly exhale with a heavy sigh. Everything about Dad is based on showing off. The sheer quantity of tasteless, gaudy decorations filling the yard is embarrassing. It's one thing if you love Christmas, but the miles of glittering tinsel, the prolific herd of reindeer, the giant Santa, and flashing lights are simply Dad saying, "Look at me! I have money!" I'm pretty sure NASA is getting a pretty good view of all this from up top, too.

For a split second, I think about retreating, pulling off, but then I remember hearing Mom's voice in the background on the call last night. "He's really coming?!"

she cried out, sounding way too excited about me making time to visit. After spending most of my life letting her down, I figure I should at least show up for an hour. Or twenty minutes. Whatever. I'll stop in and say hi for five minutes.

Stepping out of the car dad bought me, I slam the BMW door, and rub my hands together, ready to enter a warzone. The hand-written sign on the door hangs and reads, 'Five days until Santa.' I want to roll my eyes that Mom still writes the word 'Santa' on the door, since my siblings and I are definitely past the age of believing in miracles and the lies parents feed their kids. Yet, I don't roll my eyes, because it's kind of cute, Mom's belief in our youth. She's a good mom, always has been. Maybe she was too forgiving of me and my screw-ups as a kid, but it's nice to have an ally. Someone who loves me, scars and all. Too bad she married a jerk.

Dad opens the door, running his hands through his nonexistent hair, narrowing his eyes on me—but yelling so everyone else could hear within the house. "Well, look who we got over here! If it ain't my son: the *actor*." The level of disgust that rolls off his tongue makes me want to knock his ass out.

"Don't do that," I hiss, annoyed with him already.

"Do what?"

"You know what you're doing. If this is going to be a chance for you to sit around and talk crap about how I'm such a disappointment, you can save it for Christmas morning." Turning to head back to my car, I feel a hand grip into my shoulder and yank me back. When he pulls me closer to him, I smell the burnt cigar smoke that clings to his polo shirt.

"Your mother is in there waiting to see her son for the first time in a long time. So what you are going to do is smile, stand tall, and walk into the house acting like you're enjoying yourself."

That's funny coming from him, the one person who never cared about Mom or her feelings because he was too busy getting busy with other chicks who didn't have anything close to Mom's charm. What a dumbass. But after he got cancer and had his balls chopped off, he realized all he wanted to do was be with Mom, the only person who had stood by him through some of his darkest days.

It's pretty screwed up if you think about it; he had to lose his balls to grow the hell up and become a real man.

Shrugging off Dad's apparent attitude, I push myself past him and head into the living room, where the whole family is gathered. "Kayden!" Mom squeals, leaping from the couch. She hugs me longer than I let people hold me, but I don't complain. To tell you the truth, I should let her hug me a lot more often. When she pulls away, she shows her bright smile and lightly slaps my cheek. "I'm so happy to see you."

I kiss the top of her head and gently slug her on the shoulder, "It's good to see you, Ma." My eyes take a once around the space, observing everyone who's there. My older sister Katie is sitting by the coffee table playing a game of Jenga with my brother Landon and his girlfriend, Jasmine. My Uncle Randy is sleeping in the recliner while Aunt Sally is in the kitchen yapping at her two twin teenagers, Connor and Colin, to sit down and shut up.

"Boys! Video games! Upstairs, *now*!" Sally yells, and off they go running. When they leave, they shout greetings toward me, not allowing me time to respond. Sally's whole body sighs with relief, listening to the twins' voices fade away. She turns, meets my stare, and smiles. It's not long until she gives me a short hug and pulls away.

Narrowing her eyes, she taps my nose and whispers, "You smoking again?"

"Never stopped."

Nodding in silent understanding, she rolls up her sleeve and shows me the nicotine patch she's sporting.

Brave woman. "Randy wants another peanut. He must have some type of hate for me.  Look at my hair, Kay, I have gray hair. People our age shouldn't be popping out babies."

"Kids keep you young," I smirk at my aunt, whose flair for the dramatic makes her a woman after my own heart.

She rolls her eyes, pats her stomach and slaps her butt. "No, kids keep my stomach huge and my ass fat. Hailey turned seven last month and my doctor said I couldn't keep using the baby weight excuse."

"Well, what are you gonna do? Join a gym or something?"

"You kiddin' me? Hell no. I'm getting a new doctor. Clearly mine's a misogynist. Freaking creep."

Looking around, I ask, "Where is Hailey anyway?" I'm eager to see my adorable cousin, who embodies those qualities I admire most in a seven-year old kid: she's smart, sassy, and the perfect amount of rude.

"Watching those damn Disney movies in the back room." Hailey's addicted to anything and everything Disney and whenever I see her, we end up watching some princess movie over and over again. I would get annoyed by it, but it's cute the way her eyes widen as if she's seeing it for the first time.

Sally smirks again, slugs me in the arm, and walks over to Randy. “Wake your ass up, Randy! If you were just going to sleep in my brother’s chair all night and not communicate, we could’ve stayed home, saved the gas money.”

I venture over to Kate, Landon, and Jasmine, and sit in the chair across from them. Landon is the lawyer, Kate is the doctor, and I’m the actor. Guess who’s the disappointment of the bunch?

“Hey, Kayden.” Kate acknowledges me with a hello, but doesn’t look up from her intense game of Jenga. Kate is a few years older than I, and has a good head on her shoulders. She graduated a few years ago from med school and has been saving lives ever since. Our relationship is decent; it’s just that we don’t have much to talk about now that we have nothing in common.

Landon doesn’t say a word, but that’s fine, I don’t have shit to say to him either. Jasmine sits next to Landon, not looking toward me, but I know she wants to. If anything, she owes me a damn apology for what happened in the past, but I know I won’t get one any time soon. She snuggles her body closer to my brother and I let out a breath, wanting to disappear into the back room and watch Disney movies with Hailey.

“Oh! We drew secret Santa names at last Sunday’s dinner.” Mom walks over with a folded piece of paper and hands me mine. “Here ya go. Remember, over five dollars and under thirty.”

Landon releases a stiff laugh and an eye roll that’s directed toward me. “Something on your mind, Landon?” I say, leaning against the wall.

“Nope,” Landon huffs, rolling his eyes again.

I can’t stand his smugness; I feel the pressure of family life taking over and the need to escape growing stronger. “If you got something to say, get it out there.”

“Nope. Nothing. I just doubt you staying under a thirty-dollar limit will be a problem.” He reaches into his back pocket and pulls out his wallet. “Actually, here’s the five. Just so you can reach the minimum.”

I feel my fingers digging into the palms of my hands. He’s such a damn prick. “I’m good without your dirty lawyer money, bro. By the way, how are you doing, Jasmine? Landon, are you treating her right?” I spit the words out and feel a little guilty after saying them. The mocking tone is clear in my voice.

“Fuck off and get a real life, loser.” Landon grips the edge of the coffee table, knocking over the Jenga game. Kate is quick to yell, and begins to pick up the fallen pieces. Landon's words float around my head and I can't help but chuckle to myself.

If I had a penny for every time I've heard that…

Landon and I have a past that no one in the room knows about. Things we don't talk about, but it's those same things that piss us each off by just looking at one another.

"Kayden, must you be such an ass to your brother? He was trying to give you a helping hand," Dad complains, sitting on the sofa. The lawyers have to stick together I guess. "By the way, I emailed you and called three times this week. We have a position opening at the firm…"

"Not interested."

Dad arches an eyebrow and pulls out a cigar that he will probably chew on for the remainder of the night. "What?"

I don't repeat myself, because no matter what I say, he'll find a reason to disagree with it. For all these years I've been 'given a chance' to work as some lame lowly worker at Dad's law firm. The last thing I want to do is be anywhere near that place. I hate just about everything Dad loves.

"I busted my ass to get you a chance at a better life, a better future. And this is how you act? This is how you show your gratitude?"

Nothing from me. I can feel myself growing more and more pissed. He could have told me this all in private, but that wouldn't have been as entertaining for him. He prefers to have an audience when he tries to humiliate me.

"Damn actor. Actor my ass. How can you call yourself an actor if you've never even booked a job? What are you gonna do, Kayden? Bartend for the rest of your life? Knock up some random girl and end up paying child support you can't afford?"

"Fuck off," I finally say, blinking my eyes shut and trying to control my temper. I wish I didn't allow them to get under my skin so much.

"Yeah well, we'll see. Either you book an acting gig, come work for me, or find your own damn way to pay your rent. I'm sick of this, Kayden! Look at you! What are you doing with your life? Kate and Landon have their act together, and I'm giving you a free pass. A chance to get started at something. You need to let this acting thing go. It wasn't even your dream really. You're just following after Penny's—"

"Dad, don't." Kate whispers, looking up from her game. "You didn't have to bring up Penny, Dad," she states, not able to stay out of the argument due to her overdose of compassion.

"Stay out of this, Kate." I order, feeling a bit lightheaded from the mere mention of Penny. My fists clutch and my body begins to heat up, sweat crawling around the edges of my forehead. Moving to Dad, I stand before him, fearing for my life that there's a small part of him that lives within me. "I never asked for your help."

"You don't deserve my help, kid. Grow up already!"

"*Boys*!" Mom hisses, and sighs, her eyebrows frowning in displeasure. She's shaking, her small frame almost in hysterics, and immediately I feel guilty, hearing her trembling voice. "Stop, okay? Stop. Please? It's almost Christmas."

She's right. It's Christmastime, and yet another reason for the success stories of my siblings and the struggle stories of me to be brought up. Opening the piece of paper for my secret Santa I cuss under my breath, reading my brother's name on it. Karma's a bitch, and she's after me. Crumbling up my paper, I toss it into the garbage can and head toward the backyard, desperately in need of some air.

I haven't even taken off my winter coat, and I'm already in need of air. How messed up is that?

"Mmm, that smells so good." Aunt Sally peeks her head outside the screen door to find me sitting on the back patio step smoking a cig, and staring out into nothingness. "Mind if I join you?"

I've been sitting here for a few minutes, running my fingers across the engagement ring my late grandmother gave to me six years ago. I take it everywhere I go, looking at it each day, wondering what it truly stands for, wondering if it's always going to be in my possession. Sliding the ring back into my pocket, I wipe off some of the snow on the step, and pat a spot for my aunt to join me. "Course not."

She moves outside with her winter coat wrapped around her and shivers as she sits next to me. Closing her eyes, she breathes in deeply, taking in the toxic smells of tobacco. I would offer her a hit, but I know how much she wants another baby, even if she denies it. People don't put on the patch because their husbands say so. People don't put on the patch because the family hates the smells. People put on the patch because they believe there's something out there more worthwhile than a few minutes of solitude. People put on the patch because in their hearts, they want to feel more with each breath they take, every pump of their lungs.

Sometimes I wish I had a reason to wear the patch; but, as long as I'm a screw up, I'll find a reason to light up.

"What's the deal with you and Landon anyway?" Sally asks. It's a question filled with too many explanations. I shrug it off, blow a cloud smoke into the chilled air, and laugh when I see Sally try to catch the smoke in her mouth.

"Your mom's so happy you're here," she smiles and stares out into the backyard, noticing the absurd Christmas lights, yet she doesn't mention it. "She worries you know, about how you're doing. She wonders if you're all right."

"I know."

"Are you, though? Are you all right, kiddo?"

Another shrug. I'm not sure if I know what being 'all right' means. I turned twenty-seven a few months ago and drive a car my dad paid for, live in an apartment he pays half the rent for, and bartend to pay the other half. No matter how much I've tried to get myself out there in the world of acting, I haven't caught a break here in Chicago.

How do you even start building a résumé if the only way to get a part is based on your nonexistent résumé?

"I'm good."

She smiles and lays her head on my shoulder. "For an actor you're a shitty liar. Oh P.S., guess who picked you for secret Santa." Sally reaches into her coat pocket and hands me a piece of paper. "I know it's early and way less than five dollars, but fuck it. You know how I feel about rules and shit."

Narrowing my eyes, I open up the folded paper, and am taken back. My eyes shoot back to my aunt and she's still smiling. "You kidding me?"

"Merry Christmas, buddy."

The paper holds the name of a lady I'm supposed to meet tomorrow at one in the afternoon for a chance to sign with their acting agency. Not just any agency, but Walter and Jack's Talent Agency, one of the top agencies in the city. I look at Sally, no words coming to mind. My body reacts to the letter though; my hands become shaky and my feet begin tapping against the step. Running my hand across my face, trying to bite back the tears, I release a deep-gutted sigh.

"How? What…? Sally, you don't know what this means to me."

She leans in and smiles. “I do. But don’t thank me. It was actually your mom who got in touch with Stacey, who goes to the same church as we do. She’s the one you’re meeting with. Your mom fed her your sob story and she fell for it. Stacey’s also all kinds of pregnant and hormonal, so I’m sure that helped the cause.”

`”Mom did this?” I hold the paper, shocked a bit. This time my hand runs across my face and wipes actual tears away.

“Listen, kid. Just because one of your parents—my lame brother—is an ass doesn’t mean they both are. After what happened with Penny, we know it’s been hard on you, ya know? But your mom, she believes in you more than you believe in yourself. So I don’t know, maybe think about showing up for a Sunday dinner every now and then?”

I put out the cigarette, and Sally pushes off the step and heads back inside. Digging into my jacket, I pull out a piece of gum and pop it into my mouth. Turning to look inside, I see Mom joking around with Sally and my gut tightens up.

I should’ve made time for Sunday dinners.

Walking back into the house, I see Mom putting the finishing touches on her meal. She always outdoes herself, making these huge meals for people who hardly ever appreciate them. I know I never really did. Moving over to her, I wrap my arms around her tiny body and squeeze her tight. She doesn't respond with words, but she holds me right back.

"Sally told you?" she whispers. I hold her tighter, and she edges away, looking into my eyes, "I couldn't care less if you are a doctor or a lawyer, or a freaking garbage man. The only thing I want is for you to be happy, Kayden." Her eyes tear up and her hands lie over her heart. "I can promise you there's nothing worse in this world than being a mother and seeing your kid suffer. No matter their age. If this acting thing makes you happy then it makes me happy. All right?"

I smile and nod once. "All right."

"Good." She pushes me away from her and points toward the living room. "Now go hate your brother and your dad some more. It wouldn't be a holiday without all of your stupid attitudes."

Moving over to the stove, I breathe in the delicious foods. Taking my finger, I go to taste one of her many sauces heating up and she slaps my hand. "No! That one has pecans in it, and I'm not interested in killing you today. Try the one in the back I made for you."

Listening to her order, I do as I'm told and it tastes as fantastic as always. There's really nothing like Ma's cooking.

I *really* should make time for Sunday dinners.

The rest of the night runs pretty smoothly, because my mind is focused on nailing the interview tomorrow. Dad and Landon make their normal, offensive remarks about me, but I don't give a shit. Tomorrow everything changes, tomorrow my life begins.

Tomorrow, I prove them all wrong.

After a night spent at my parents' house, I am more determined than ever to ace this audition. But the longer I sit across from this pregnant lady who looks like she's five, the more I feel like a failure. She tugs on her ear, browsing over my less-than-amusing résumé, which forces me to shift around in my chair.

"So, Mr. Reece, you've been acting for—?"

"A few years. Mainly looking for a way to break into the business, to get a chance to show what I can do."

She nods, muttering to herself as she continues looking at the résumé with a look of displeasure. Setting the resume aside, she lifts her head to give me a benign, kind smile that does little to disguise the pity she feels as she searches for the right words to let me down gently. "You have a great look, you really do. A fresh face, nice voice. But—"

There's always a 'but'.

"But, your experience is a bit lacking. Perhaps work now on building your résumé, getting more experience. When you do that, come back and see me again."

I hear my Dad in my ears, echoing how I'm a loser and need to get a real job. Placing my hands on the edges of her desk, I search for a voice that sounds confident and not beggarly. "Mrs. Ericks, I can do this. I know I can be a big benefit to your agency, and I know I will benefit from your agency's representation. I get it—I lack the impressive credentials you are looking for. I didn't study theater at the top schools, or lock in my first commercial at the age of three. But this is what I want. This is who I am. From the bottom of my soul, I promise you better than my best. I promise you the top of the line. I won't disappoint you, and failure is not an option. There's something inside me telling me I'm in the right place. This is supposed to be my home. All I need you to do is invite me in."

She's quiet for a moment, staring at me with eyes that are filling with emotion. *She's giving in. She's going to let me in.*

Suddenly, her office door bursts open and a woman wearing way too much make-up stumbles in, her face pale. Even with the make-up she looks freaking awful. "Stacey—sorry to interrupt. We are swamped out here with auditions for the toothpaste commercial and I have—" Her hand flies to her mouth as a gagging sounds comes out and her body starts to quiver. Shifting quickly to the garbage can, the lady starts upchucking her lunch, breakfast, and the rest of the week's menu.

"Oh my gosh. Grace! Go home!" Stacey stands, and moving closer to her co-worker, checks to see if she's all right as she ushers her toward the door.

*No! Come back! You were just about to sign me!*

"Mr. Reece." Stacey turns to me and gives me a sad grin. "Thank you for coming in. Remember, when you get those additional résumé builders please, stop by again. In the front lobby there is some information on acting classes and headshots from photographers. Please hang out for as long as you wish."

No. *No!* Rejection. Failure. Loser. Dismissal.

Walking out of the office, I hang around in the lobby for a while, watching real actors coming in for real auditions. I sit there, pretending to be one of them, make believing. I don't go home right away, because the moment I walk out of this building, I know my once-in-a-lifetime shot at a real acting career will be nothing more than a memory.

# 2 Jules

## The Trouble with Boys

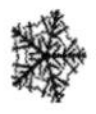

"Ms. Peterson, no offense, but I'm not going to let you win this time. Oh, did I tell you about my family trip coming up?" I exhale noisily, moving my checker pieces across the board.

On Thursdays I always take a half-day from work so I can volunteer at the Outers Retirement home. Nursing homes just so happen to smell like a million of grandparents' homes all at once; kind of like a mixture of candy and liniment. I love coming to Outers; the people here are so amazing to interact with in this place. It's so important to give back to the community, remembering that the elderly need love too and…Ah hell.

Really I come here to complain about my dysfunctional family because all my friends and co-workers are sick of hearing about it. The old people don't care either, but most of the time they are just happy to have someone playing checkers with them. I would play chess—but do I look like Einstein? Trust me, I don't look like Einstein.

“I mean, I’m trying my best not to think about it too much, and there’s not much I can do to take away from the awkwardness of it all, but well, here we are.” I sigh and double jump the red checker chip over the black. “Do you think I’m overthinking it? Mom said I’m overthinking it, but let’s be honest. She also said I was overthinking the fact that Danny wasn’t going to propose and look at us now.” My eyes shift to my ringless finger and an unattractive, heavy frown takes over my lips. Mom should have named me Pathetic. It seems more fitting.

I look up to the old woman sitting across from me, who is smiling wide and nodding in response. Happy listeners are the best listeners, so I keep on yapping. “I know what you’re thinking. Why didn’t the jerk propose? Well, probably because he was too busy getting it on with my nasty ho-bag of a sister. There are so many days I wish I had a sibling redo. I wish I could take her and push her back into Mom’s va-jay-jay and get another sister. A real sister, not a ho-bag sister.” The elderly woman smiles even bigger and nods some more.

I bite my bottom lip, grinding my teeth into my flesh and narrow my eyes. “Did you forget to put in your hearing aids, Ms. Peterson?” No response other than a big fake dentures smile and nodding. “Perfect. Anyway, at least this time I have someone to take home with me for the Christmas weekend at the cabin. Mom kept reminding me about the fact that I've ditched the last three years and she guilt-tripped me by saying Grandma probably doesn't have many more years with us because she's as old as a bat—no offense."

Nod. Smile. Smile. Nod.

"Besides, this Christmas is going to be special." Reaching into my coat pocket, I pull out a ring box and watch Ms. Peterson's eyes widen with joy. Leaning in toward her I whisper, "Richard's going to propose!"

"HA!" is the sound that travels to my ears from old man Eddie, who's sitting at a table across the room. "Sunshine, how do you know a man's going to propose? Either he does or he doesn't!"

"Shut it, Eddie. He left it under the bed this morning."

"You mean he *dropped* it under the bed this morning." Eddie snickers as he rolls his wheelchair over to the table, joining Ms. Peterson and me.

Rolling my eyes I shrug my shoulders. "Po-tay-to! Po-tah-to! Whatever! I'm engaged!"

"He didn't ask you."

I frown, staring at the sparkling, somewhat underwhelming diamond. "Must you put such a damper on this?"

"Listen sweetheart, you've been dating this guy for what, seven months? He's not the one. And when you've been around as long as I have, you realize that you should let them go and not waste your time. He's not for you."

Running the ring through my fingers I sigh, "He's the one for me. Not everyone can be like you and Ms Peterson."

Ms. Peterson laughs as Eddie takes her hand into his and kisses it, making her instantly transform into a high school teenager. They met each other a few years ago here and are the main couple of the nursing home. Ms. Peterson has been known to beat off other women who give Eddie googly eyes. I appreciate her ability to mark her territory, as it's something I wish I could have done in my past.

"Julie Anne, the loser's idea of date night is ordering Chinese food and having you watch him play something about calling and duties all night long."

I hate when Eddie uses my full name. It makes it seem like he's scolding me. "I like those nights. Besides, he's finally ready to meet my family. He's coming to Wisconsin with me. I think he's going to propose in front of my parents!"

Eddie groans at my words and slaps his hand against his face—for extra insult. "Let's think about this. We all know you rush into relationships."

"I do not!"

"Do too!" is heard throughout the whole community hall from all of the people who live in the nursing home. If I weren't so awkward, I may have even been offended.

Eddie smiles to me and rubs the bald spot on his head. "Peter the computer geek, Ryan the drug addict, and don't even get us started on Tyler the personal trainer."

"They weren't that bad."

"Ha! Tyler had you working out five times a day. And I think we both know how you feel about gyms. It's a nasty sweatshop that makes…"

I mutter, "…women feel inferior to men. Yes, okay. So in the past I haven't picked out the best guys. But Richard is different. This ring shows that!"

"Ah to be young and an idiot again." Eddie grins and kisses Ms. Peterson's hand. She is of course nodding and smiling. "The truth is you never got over that asshole Danny."

"That's not fair. He was the love of my life…" I explain, hoping to change the subject.

Eddie's mood shifts as he leans in toward me and places his hand over mine. "Sunshine, the love of your life wouldn't cheat on you with your sister."

He's right. I definitely hate him for being right, but mostly I hate myself for still missing Danny, even though I now have a Richard.

"Alright, well, I think I've suffered enough for one visit. I gotta stop by the agency, pick up some liquor to hide in my sock drawer like in high school, and then hit the road." Standing from my victorious game of checkers with Ms. Peterson, I give Eddie a hug and receive a kiss on the cheek from the handsome gentleman. I walk around and kiss the elderly woman on the top of her head. "Merry Christmas you two."

"Happy Easter, dear," Ms. Peterson says, holding up her middle finger and kissing her lips against it.

"Happy Christmas, Jules! And congratulations on your bubble gum machine diamond." Eddie laughs and laughs, with Ms. Peterson joining in. I watch her pull out her hearing aids and stick them in. *She was ignoring me on purpose!* After picking up my stunned jaw from the floor I head out toward the acting agency to grab some packets before my five-hour trip to upper Wisconsin.

"Oh my gosh, Jules, I'm so glad you're here! We are swamped! First, fast question, do my feet look swollen?" Stacey, my co-worker, steps out of her slip-on shoes and shows me her fat toes. Ew. She sure knows how to make pregnancy look appealing. "Gross, right? Anyway, please say you'll stay and help me with these auditions."

"No Stace! I was just stopping by to pick up a few things. I have a five-hour drive with Richard starting in less than an hour to go watch my sister tongue the ex-love of my life. I can't help this time," I cry at my begging co-worker as I walk into the agency to see a room filled with hopeful male actors who are auditioning for the new Fresh toothpaste commercial. "P.S. I'm still pissed at you for ignoring the picture of Richard I sent you last night. He looked super hot."

Stacey's eyebrows arch. "You didn't send me a picture."

"Right. Lie about it. Whatever, I gotta get going."

"No! Please, Jules! We are hours behind, Grace went home with food poisoning, Claire is knee-deep in audition applications, and I'm eight-and-a-half months pregnant, hungry as fuck, and annoyed as hell." Stacey wobbles into my office—well, my boss's office, which I am using until his vacation is over—with her large puppy-dog eyes staring me down. No lie, Stacey makes a super cute preggers woman, but her begging isn't going to help. I still have to pack! Plus there's supposed to be this crazy blizzard moving in.

"Sorry, babes." Shrugging my shoulders, I reach into my pocket, pull out the engagement ring, and exclaim, "Richard has a big weekend planned for us!" Expecting an excited response in return from my friend, my high-pitched pronouncement is met instead with a silent stare at the ring box.

"What is that?" She asks, narrowing her eyes. "Where's the diamond? And why are you even considering marrying him? Everyone knows you're only taking him up to your family's cabin to show Danny that you're over him. Which in turn makes it quite obvious that you are *not* over Danny."

A huff falls from me and I pull the ring away from her viewpoint. "You're a mean pregnant woman. Did you know that? Anyway, I'm leaving now, and the next time you see me, I will be back as a fiancée! Happy holidays!"

Picking up my paperwork, I turn away from my rude co-worker, and head out of the room, still staring at the diamond ring. It's gorgeous! It's pretty. It's nice. *Sigh…it's decent.*

Walking through the agency in my own world, I envision my future wedding—the colors, the flowers, the look of shock on my family's faces, Danny's nonexistent body because he's not invited—and I am shaken from my daydream when my body slams against a wall…a moving wall, with *abs*? My eyes look up to an outrageously handsome man standing in front of me, who I almost plowed over. My papers go flying everywhere, and the engagement ring lands across the room, yet I have to force myself to break contact with his green eyes, which are firmly locked with mine. I shake my head back and forth, repeating Richard's name in my mind. *Richard, Richard! I'm engaged to Richard!*

"Oh no!" I overreact, looking at my papers and the soon-to-be-on-my-finger ring resting on the carpeted floor.

The handsome guy helps me, apologizing for not paying attention; but, now I'm a little worried about my ring that went flying. That's a five thousand dollar ring!

Okay, maybe one thousand. Five hundred? Hell, okay I saw the same one for two hundred and fifty dollars at Walmart during Black Friday, whatever.

Bending down to pick up the ring, handsome guy beats me to it; and I am lost in the moment as he's down on one knee, holding the ring up to me. My mind melts, forcing me to lose all my common sense. "*I do*!" I scream. His brows raise, and my hands fly over my lips, "I mean *I do* need to get going with that." Awkward laughter starts now, but I don't know if it's coming from him or me.

When he hands it to me, he smiles this stunning grin; he must definitely be an actor auditioning for the toothpaste commercial. "Congratulations on your engagement."

"Oh, I'm not engaged, yet. But he did this really cute thing this morning; it's a pretty darn adorable story actually..." I laugh, and the stranger stares at me with a blank expression, waiting for me to share. "Okay, well, I woke up, and found out that he left the ring under my bed for me to discover."

A short laugh escapes his almost closed lips, "You mean he dropped it under your bed?"

"Ugh! What is it with people and all of these stupid technicalities?" I mutter, snatching the ring from his hands.

His smile grows bigger, and I would almost hate his smugness if his eyes weren't all sultry and dreamy.

"Well, good luck with that." He turns away to walk back over to the lobby and my hands land on my hips.

"I don't need your luck! I *am* getting engaged! It's a done deal pretty much. So screw you, and the old people, and my mother, and my sister, and Danny, and all of your stupid technicalities which have nothing to do with me and my *soon-to-be husband*!" I shout.

When everyone in the room pauses and stares at me as if I grew another head, I know it's time to leave. I rush outside toward my 1999 Honda, ready to hit the road to my apartment. "Keys keys…" I jumble my hands through my tiny purse—which I bought because I thought it would keep me from losing crap. What a lie.

The roads are a bit slippery, but the hardcore snow storm isn't suppose to hit until midnight, which is exactly why I want to jump in the car with my honey, hit the road, and travel down the highway to hell.

I open my apartment door, ready to rub Richard all up in nasty Danny's and Lisa's faces. "Babes, I'm back! Stacey tried to get me to stay at the office but I told her how overly nervous I am about taking you back home with me to meet the folks. Did you pack our toothbrushes?

That's okay, I'll grab them." I see Richard moving around in the living room, fidgeting back and forth, searching through the sofa cushions. My heart smiles when I see him on the hunt for what I believe is in my coat pocket.

"I already know," I whisper, and he turns toward me, crossing his arms across his chest. His eyebrow arches and he waits for me to explain. I smile, pulling out the engagement ring. "I think it's sweet. I know this isn't the way you probably wanted this to go, but that's okay. I'm fine with this."

A heavy sigh falls from his lips and he runs his hands through his hair. "Jules, I was having panic attacks here! I thought you would be so pissed! We both knew this wasn't going anywhere, right? I mean, we met as I was leaving a strip club with my buddies." He heads for the bedroom and I follow after him, all kinds of confused.

"Wait, what are you talking about?" I pause. "You said you were only at the strip club for your friend's bachelor party."

He gives me such a strong you-are-freaking-stupid look and I sigh. I *am* freaking stupid. Of course he wasn't at a bachelor party.

"I'm leaving, sweets." He rubs his chin and shoots his chocolate eyes my way. The same eyes that made me fall head over heels for him in the first place. The same eyes I got lost in every day for the past seven months. The same eyes that I gave a key to my apartment!

"I beg your pardon?" I say. Richard really has to work on his comedic timing, because this isn't funny.

He sits on the edge of the bed and he gives me a halfway grin that pisses me off. "I just feel like I'm at the age where I'm ready to settle down, you know? And yesterday Hanna and I were talking about kids, and I think I'm ready for that next step."

Hanna?

He pushes himself off of the bed and walks over to me. "I was freaking out when I realized I lost the ring, but I can always count on you." He slugs me in the arm. No lie—*he actually slugs me in the arm!*

"What the hell are you talking about, Richard?!"

"I'm asking my girlfriend of four years to marry me."

A flood of witty remarks from my mom start flying through my head. The disappointment in Grandma's face at her still single granddaughter, with no babies, paints pictures in my mind. Dad…he's going to get drunk and laugh at me. Come to think of it, Grandma's going to get drunk and laugh at me, too. And then there will be Lisa and Danny, holding each other, kissing each other…

"NO!" I hiss, rubbing my hands across my face, my blood boiling. I see Richard pick up his luggage and move toward the door. I block his only way out. "No, Richard!" His eyes fall on me, confused by my anger. Fuck him! He just ruined my life.

"Jules, baby..." he whispers, trying to edge his way around me.

I grip the sides of the door frame, shaking with such serious amounts of frustration. "You are *not* ditching me twenty minutes before we hit the road to meet my family."

No. No! This isn't happening. I reserved an extra plate for the table at the cabin *for my boyfriend*! I bought two hundred dollars worth of video games *for my boyfriend*! I spent over six hundred dollars on a new video game system *for my boyfriend*! God dammit I earned the right to tie this asshole up, drag the son-of-a-bitch outside, and toss him into my car trunk next to my unopened Pilates DVDs while playing loud Christmas carols and driving in absurd amounts of snowfall.

"Jules, sweets...you're a little scary right now. There's like some weird wrinkles in your forehead." Richard frowns at my appearance, and I can't blame him. If I look as crazed as I feel, he should really rethink leaving.

"Listen, Richard. I am freaking out. I have pimples in places where pimples should never be. I am going home after three years of avoiding that fucking cabin. I'm pissy, I'm stressed, and I am *not* the person you want to cross right now. I get it. You're a liar. You're a cheater. You're a bad lay. But right now? Right now, I don't give a damn. You are getting in that car—*now*! I'm not kidding, you little shit. I.Will.Cut.A.Bitch." I growl at him, watching his eyes fill with fear.

"Uh, just to be clear... The bitch in this situation…?" he questions.

"You. You're the bitch, Richard."I warn him with a look filled with death. He's so lucky I don't have superpowers, because he would be dead in an alley somewhere.

Swinging his way under my arms, he squeezes through. "I'm sorry, Jules. I really am. But I'm gonna give you some time to calm your nerves. Then I'll pick up the rest of my stuff."

Slam.

He's gone. He's gone and I am past due for a mental meltdown. Oh my gosh, how can I do it? How can I go back to that cabin to see my sister, my one true love, and their love child together?

So…ugly crying has been happening for the past twenty minutes, Hall and Oates *She's Gone* is on repeat, and the gut-wrenching realization that I set myself up for yet another disappointing relationship is slowly sinking into my spirit. What's wrong with me? Why do I fall for the ones who will never dive in for me?

Hearing my phone ring, I rush over to it, hoping to hear Richard say 'December Fools,' and tell me this is some kind of sick prank he's playing on me and that he's really loading the car up downstairs. Unfortunately it's not Richard. Oh how I wish it *were* the cheating liar. I listen to the ringing phone for a few seconds more, debating if I really want to answer.

"Hey Mom," I say in the most upbeat tone. If she hears a crack in my voice, she'll know something is up and hold it against me for the rest of my life.

"Hey, honey! Just calling to see if you two hit the road yet…"

Glancing out of my kitchen window down to the street, I see where Richard's car was previously parked. Nothing but an emptied space. "Uh—yup. Richard just pulled the car out of the parking structure."

"Oh, he's driving? Wonderful. You know how your driving gets on icy roads." Insult number one: check. "Let me speak to him really fast. I want to know if he wants chicken or fish for Christmas Eve dinner. Tonight I think we'll just have the homemade pizzas. So let me ask him."

"Fish. He wants fish, Mom."

"Any allergies? Let me speak to him."

"Nope, no need to talk to him. He's as healthy as a fox and allergy free!"

"Lord, Julie. You could have let me speak to him on my own. You do know that at one point he'll have to talk to us, seeing how he'll be standing in front of us in a few hours."

No. He won't.

"I know, Mom. It's just, he's driving."

"Your sister and Danny arrived earlier. To tell you the truth, Lisa didn't think you were really bringing a guy. For awhile, I agreed." Insult number two: check.

"Gee, thanks. Well, for your information, we are on our way right now." Oh my gosh. I don't have a boyfriend. *I don't have a boyfriend!*

"Well, I'm glad. Little Olivia could really use a cousin sometime soon. Your eggs aren't getting any younger, and

I really hope you will look into that email I sent you about freezing them."

Ding ding ding! We have a winner! Three insults in less than three minutes! Somebody get the lady a prize!

"Oh?! What's that, Mom?! I'm losing you!" Covering the receiver I make the best static sounds known to mankind. "We—in—tunnel. See—later. B—y—e." Hitting end on a telephone call never felt so good. Then it sets in. I told Mom that Richard wanted fish, which he doesn't. He doesn't want anything other than Hanna and her nonexistent babies. I hate Hanna and her nonexistent babies.

"Breathe… Just breathe…" I fall to the floor and do some major rocking back and forth, gasping for air, grasping for answers. "What am I going to do? What am I going to?" My eyes move to the paperwork I brought in from the agency and I pause. And this wave of energy rocks through my spirit, sending me powerful bursts of a plan. Maybe I *am* Einstein!

"Jules! What are you doing back here?" Stacey asks, following my fast pace into the front lobby with all of the actors.

"Richard broke up with me to marry his girlfriend of four years." I mutter and the look of non-shock from Stacey pierces me. "What?! You saw this coming?"

"Well, not exactly this. But, you do have a history of picking up losers."

I don't reply because she's not wrong. She sounds just like Eddie. "Anyway, I need help. I need to steal an actor."

Stacey raises an eyebrow, placing both of her hands under her ever-growing belly. "What do you mean you need to steal an actor?"

"No time to explain."

"Okay, whatever. I have to go get food before I burn this place down and eat people's ankles, but first, feel that." She grabs my hands and places them on her stomach, where a weird vibration happens. I try my best not to make a grossed-out face, but I can't help it. That felt freaking nasty. Stacey nods. "I know right? The joys of pregnancy."

With that, she turns away and wobbles out of the building. Going back to the front lobby, I walk in front of all of the male actors in the room and stand up on one of the chairs. “I am in need of an actor for a five-day trip to my parents’ cabin to pretend to be my boyfriend.”

The room is filled with silence, all types of green, blue, and brown eyes staring at me with the blankest of blank expressions.

“I’ll pay you one thousand dollars to be my made-up boyfriend. Five days.”

Crickets. Freakin’ A! “Okay, let’s be honest shall we? There’s a .00005 chance that you will land the role for Fresh toothpaste today. This dude over here has eyebrows that are too caterpillar-like. This kid looks like he’s fifteen. And you”—I point to the guy in the corner, giving me a rude look— “you have a nose that would only be featured in a sinus and cold commercial. So if you want to pass up an opportunity to get paid money for eating cookies, opening presents, and hating my sister, then fine. Pass it up. But truthfully, one thousand dollars for acting is more than some of you will make in a year.”

A guy in the back says something, but I can’t see or hear him. I clear my throat, and stand on my tiptoes. “Who said something?”

Out of nowhere this tall, dark figure stands from his chair and steps up. He has beautiful brown hair, perfectly styled facial hair and a jaw line that makes my thighs clench and my lady parts scream, "*Hallelujah!*"

"I said, do we get paid half up front?"

When we lock eyes, I can feel my cheeks redden, because he's the same stranger who picked up the engagement ring for me earlier. He comes to the same realization, and that smile of his widens the same way it did earlier.

"Well, we can work something out." I blink, but only once, because I want to take in his green eyes for as long as possible. He's wearing a white button-down shirt that is hiding his clearly toned body. "What's your name?"

"Kayden Reece."

"Why don't I know you?" I know all of our clients. It's my job to file, file, and file some more of their paperwork.

"I was signed on to the team this afternoon. This is my first official audition."

Ohh, he's sexy. I can use fresh meat; they are less likely to ask for a raise. "Age?"

"Twenty-seven."

Ohhh, older than me by a year. Perfect! "Girlfriend?"

He shifts his glance to the ground and I can tell he's smiling. An overwhelming amount of desire fills me when he looks up again and I get to take in the smile. It's sexy and adorable all at one. Sexdorable. His smile is so sexdorable it almost kills me. If I didn't have a thing against dating actors, and if my heart weren't currently being dragged through the mud, I would totally be up for making some babies with him.

His looks alone make Danny appear like the ugliest man alive, which pleases me quite a bit, but that's not all he has that is so much more charming than Danny. Kayden has this deep, sultry, smoky voice that pulls all of the attention to him whenever he speaks. Danny sounds like freaking Mickey Mouse on crack. Kayden also has this edgy characteristic about him that reads badass yet sweetheart all at once. And with a name like Kayden, he was destined to be all kinds of yum.

"No girlfriend to claim at this moment in time."

I nod once and step off of the chair, giving an evil glance to all of the actors who didn't step up for the role of a lifetime. "Follow me to my office, Mr. Reece."

"I'm guessing the proposal didn't go over too great?" Kayden asks, and my gut tightens. I don't reply, and watch as he shifts around in his chair. Clearly he knows now that he should've kept that comment to himself.

"So, here's the thing. I can pay you five hundred dollars upfront. You'll get the rest after we leave Haven Creeks, Wisconsin. You can stop by your place, pack up some things. If you have any white or black winter wear, that would be perfect. Then we can match and be super cute and like a match made in heaven. Then again, I bought a few hats and gloves for the ass whose name shall not be spoken, so I'll pack that up for you, too." I scatter papers around my desk, looking for something, anything, just to avoid looking at the beautiful piece of man candy sitting across from me. He's smirking, which in turn makes my lady parts smirk. *He knows he's good-looking. He has to!*

"Ms. Stone," he cuts in and I hold my hand up.

"Oh God no. My mom is Mrs. Stone, I'm Jules, please."

"All right, Jules. I'm sorry, this is all happening pretty fast. So, is there a way we can start from the beginning?" I stop my shuffling and look at the handsome man sitting across from me. He's leaning forward, running his hand across his chin.

I feel my cheeks heat up, feeling silly that this sudden plan of mine is actually a load of crap. My head falls to the desk and I curse under my breath. When my head rises, I can tell that my curly blond hair looks like hell, but I don't care about much anymore.

"Listen, I'm a hot mess and this is insanely unprofessional, but it's also very much like me because I'm a nut job. This isn't even my office. It's my boss's, but he's gone on vacation with his wife, who loves him. I work in the cubicle in the back corner." I try to fight the tears that are thrusting their way to the surface. "I come to work every day, happy to help people reach their dreams because I didn't reach mine. Everyone in my family are freaks. My sister's a whore who I oddly enough wish I could be. And I date losers because I think that's all I can attract." My bottom lip starts to tremble, and the tears of a sad, single girl start spilling from my eyes. "And my only friends are ninety-year-olds who have more make-out sessions than I do!"

Ignite ugly crying now.

I sob into my hands and proceed to get all snotty and gross in front of Sir Hottie-Smiles.

"Um, Jules, is everything okay?" Claire peeks her head in my office, forcing me to cry even harder because it's not okay. Nothing's okay. I don't look up at her because she has a fiancé and she's happy and younger than me, which adds insult to injury.

"I think she'll be okay," Kayden says, making me peek my eyes through my fingers to find him staring at me. It's intimidating how he looks at me, because it's not like he simply stares. It's more like he can see into me. See my spirit, my soul, which is worrisome because if he sees that deep into me then he would be running away any minute now.

Claire looks over to me, and I nod to her through my tears. She slowly closes the office door, locking Kayden and me inside. Kayden moves from his chair and holds his hand out toward me. "Can I try something?" he requests, waiting for me to give him my hand. I look at my hands—all snotty and nastified—and wipe them against my jeans.

Kayden takes my hand, pulls me up from my sob party for one, and walks me to the door. Positioning my back against it, he takes my other hand into his. His proximity to my body is extremely close and somewhat petrifying. The cold wood from the door touches the back of my neck, creating powerful shivers. He positions himself in front of me, his body demanding my attention. He's at least six-foot-four, which makes me appear short at five-foot-eight.

Is he going to kiss me? Because I'm not going to kiss him. *I don't even know you!*

"I'm not going to kiss you," he explains.

*Oh.* My lips frown for a moment, but I hope he doesn't notice.

"Well, not yet at least. Close your eyes."

"Kayden, I understand you really want this job but let's forget about it. It's a stupid idea and it's hardly a real acting job. How about an 'IOU'? I promise you another audition for a great role and…" I argue all of the reasons why this actor shouldn't be hovering over me, and I'm pretending to try to pull away. Truth is, I really want to pull him closer and have him press against my body, allowing him to slowly introduce his tongue to mine. He raises an eyebrow toward me; I arch one back and sigh, closing my eyes.

His face presses against mine. The scratchiness of his beard brushes against me as my hands fall to my sides. "Stop comparing yourself to your sister." His hands slide to my lower back, and before I have the power to go weak, he tightens his hold, pulling me closer to him. When I hear him mention my sister, I go to open my eyes but he stops me. "Keep them shut. You're nothing like her. And she's nothing like you. Forgot about all of the losers who didn't know what type of treasure they let get away. They don't exist anymore. No one on this planet does. It's just you and me for these five days. There's nothing to worry about. No commitment. No planning. Just us and our holiday."

I can feel his lips mere millimeters away from mine as the words roll off of his tongue with such ease. For a minute, I forget we are standing in my office—er, my boss's office—and that my mascara is still running down my cheeks. I forget we met five minutes ago when I offered to pay someone an obscene amount of money to be my made-up boyfriend. I forget who Richard, Danny, and Lisa are. All I want to do is find the taste of the man with his hands around my waist.

"I'm going to kiss you now," he warns, edging his face closer to mine. "Unless you stop me."

I don't speak a word; I have no reason whatsoever to want to stop him.

When his lips find mine, I feel as if I've won the sexdorable lottery. His lips are soft, addicting, and gentle at first before the kiss grows deeper. I place my hands on his chest, stilling myself from tumbling over as his tongue slowly brushes against my lips. The way his rock-hard abs feel against my touch, makes me moan for more. My hips involuntarily rock in his direction, and he lifts me up against the door, kissing me harder, deeper, in a way that makes me feel as if we have been sharing these types of kisses for a lifetime. He allows my legs to wrap around his waist, and he holds me, making me feel so safe at his touch. His fingers stroke through my curly locks of hair, and when he pulls his mouth away from mine, I cannot help but miss his taste, his heat, his made-up passion. His eyes open to find my blues staring back at him, and he tilts my head, giving me one last kiss before I feel him smiling against my mouth. When my feet find the ground, my knees almost forget how to keep me standing, but Kayden's hand is around my back, holding me, protecting me from falling.

"Well then…" I clear my throat once, "You are a fantastic actor," I say, breathless, and emotionally drugged up on Mr. Sexdorable.

He doesn't step back, and I hold his stare, my eyes flooded with his greens. He smirks a small amount and shrugs, "I figure if we're going to do this then we should have our first kiss now instead of in front of your family. That would take away from the awkwardness of it all."

"You didn't even audition for the part yet."

His tongue runs across his lips and he moves his hand through his dark hair. "I guess I jumped the gun."

"The gun has been jumped."

We're still for quite a bit of time before I blink and realize that if this is happening then we have to hit the road before I come to my senses, wake up from this dream, or have a heart attack from how beautiful he is. I know guys don't like being called beautiful, but he is.

So. Freaking. Beautiful.

After he pulls up to my apartment, I watch him climb out of his car, suitcase in hand, wearing that same engaging smile. He's driving a deep blue BMW—something I can't imagine most struggling actors would be driving. Who is this guy? Why isn't he more weirded out by this situation? How do I know he's not a psycho killer?

Dragging my luggage down the stoned apartment steps, I pause as Kayden strides forward to help me. "I got it…" I mutter, almost breathless. Narrowing my eyes on him, I watch as he walks with me to load my car up and I swing myself around to face him. "Hey, quick question."

"Shoot."

"You're not a murderer, psychopath, or anywhere close to being a crazy person, are you?"

"Well," he sighs, "I haven't killed since last Thursday, which is a record for me. I didn't pass the psych test, but really, does anyone pass those? And crazy? Well, yes. I am. But honestly, the people you should really worry about are the ones who claim to be sane."

He's so sarcastic and snarky that all I want to do is lick his face.

I wish I weren't so weird sometimes.

"Okay, well just so you know, I have a black belt in karate, a certificate from a woman's self-defense class, and pepper spray. So that pretty much means I will kill you if you need to be killed."

"Duly noted."

"Good." I grab my keys and toss them toward, Kayden, "By the way…you're driving because my mom thinks you are. Your name is Richard, we've been dating for seven months, and you are in accounting, but you're looking to transfer over to business and marketing."

The confused look on his face is almost classic comedy, and it makes me smile.

"Don't worry; I'll fill you in on the ride up there."

I pause and look at him, not moving. I can't get in a car with this stranger, and I think he knows. He smiles again and hands me my keys. "I'll follow behind you."

"Thank you."

"Of course. But mainly it's for my own safety. I haven't been pepper sprayed in awhile, and I would rather hold on to that fact." He extends his cell phone toward me and asks me to program my phone number into it so we can talk and learn more about our 'acting adventures' on the ride up north.

Why do I have the feeling this is all going to blow up in my face?

The snow isn't falling too hard, and the drive is mostly filled with my own awkward silence with the phone against my ear and moments of me looking through my rearview mirror staring at his strikingly stunning facial structure.

"So…" he sighs into the cell phone, "what should I know about you that your family would expect me to know?"

"Oh." I straighten up in my seat, thinking of what facts my family normally mocks me with. "I'm left-handed. I went to college for a semester before dropping out and going down the road of acting. Didn't really lead to Hollywood for me, but that's all right. I like being behind the scenes, hooking people up with their dreams of the big screen."

"That's a lie," he says, as if he knows every fact about me already.

"What?"

"You gave up on acting. You settled."

"You don't even know me," I argue, somewhat taken aback by his sudden claim that he knows I gave up on acting. Which…I kind of did.

"No, I get it. It's a scary business not knowing where your next paycheck is coming from, and the older you get, the harder it becomes to explain to your friends that you haven't broken into the industry yet. But you swear all you need is one chance. The right audition to get your foot in the door. Yet somewhere in your gut you hear the words 'give up' taking over. Those words start becoming stronger each and every day, and soon even the whiskey won't tune them out. Then you're sitting in another audition for another part you won't get and you pause and wonder why you did it all. Why you missed so many birthdays, holidays, anniversaries, Sunday dinners. All for what? The love of your craft? Your passion? Let's just say I understand why some people would walk away from all of this."

"Story of your life?" I snicker, glancing in my rearview mirror toward him, but I stop laughing suddenly when I see his face tighten up and his cheeks hollow out.

"Story of my life." He runs his hand over his mouth and shakes it back and forth before losing his somewhat somber expression. "But then again, this isn't about me. It's about Richard. So, tell me more and more about this character of mine. What's my motivation?"

"Um, you're a work-a-holic. Which should have been my first warning sign…" I sigh, trying to fight back yet another wave of tears. I should have realized that Richard didn't work that late into the evenings. He was never able to hang out with me. It's all adding up, how he probably told his girlfriend he was on business conference trips when really he was seeing his mistress. Oh my gosh, I'm the mistress. This is all becoming a bad Lifetime movie. "Can we not talk about Richard?"

"We won't talk about Richard."

Perfect. I wish he weren't in his car, because talking on the phone like this is awkward. Plus, I have sweaty ear.

"Um, Jules?" he whispers into the phone.

"Yes?"

"You can put your phone on speaker, you know. Then maybe you won't swerve all over the freeway."

"What! I'm not…" A horn blows at me as a car sweeps past.

Speaker phone it is.

# 3 Kayden

## There's Something About Julie

I am a fucking asshole. I can't believe I lied about being signed to the agency, but I couldn't do it. I couldn't go back to my parents and tell them that I didn't land the agent. The smug look on Dad's face would kill me alone. I was almost certain Jules would do some kind of background check, to make sure it were true, but she hadn't. She just…cried.

This chick is crazy. It's been twenty minutes on speaker phone and she's been crying over her ex-boyfriend for the last eighteen. Plus she drives like a blind person, all over the road. Let's just say that I'm happy I'm not in her car.

My phone's volume has been on low for the last five minutes, because I can't listen to her 'Oh woe is me, I'm in my mid-twenties and single while my hot younger sister has a baby with the ex-love of my life.' She really needs to work on her communication skills with strangers, because she has really laid out all of her life problems to me in two minutes.

I've dated girls like her—or well, I've at least slept with them. The cling-aholics. They do just about anything to keep a guy from leaving them, which makes us want to run even faster. I noticed the look of desperation when I kissed her. Don't get me wrong—surprisingly she has to be one of the top three best kisses of my life. Her lips are gentle and full and they taste like strawberries. But the look in her eyes after we pulled away is what scared me shitless. She looked at me as if we were an item. A *real* item—not this made-up relationship thing.

I don't even know why I agreed to this. I guess I want an opportunity to shove it in my dad's face. To say I booked a job, to say I'm on the right path. For me not giving a damn what he thinks of me, I hate how I try so damn hard to prove him wrong.

Hitting the volume up, I hear Jules still whining. Great. Back into my acting role… "Look, Jules. I don't think you give yourself enough credit. You deserve better than these guys. You need to set rules for yourself."

I can already tell that she hops into bed with any guy who looks at her for more than a minute while already planning the wedding. For someone who's in her twenties, she sure acts like a teenager. But truth be told, most chicks do. I blame Disney and their fake Prince Charmings.

If I've learned anything from watching movies with Hailey, it's pretty clear Prince Charming is gay. He's definitely more interested in Cinderella's high heels than he is in sleeping with her. And if he isn't gay, all of his sweet talk is just to get her out of that dress and into his bed. The only dude I have any respect for is the guy who tried to get Belle to marry him by threatening to send her dad to the psych ward. At least he was up front with what he was after. He pretty much said, 'Listen, I'm hot as hell. You're hot as hell. I have great hair. Your hair is all right. Let's shack up, make some babies, and then call it a day.'

"You think so? You think I need rules?" Her voice pulls me out of my thoughts and back into the conversation—a conversation I'm sure is pointless. Most girls never listen to advice, even when they ask for it.

"I know so."

"Like what kind of rules?" Her voice is timid, cute even, because the idea of setting guidelines for dating makes her so nervous.

"For example, maybe you shouldn't sleep with the guy just because he calls you beautiful. Or because he winks at you. Or because he buys you a drink."

There's a short gasp heard through the phone line. "How did you know about the winking?"

"Sweetheart, we all know about the winking. And it's clear that you're beautiful, but that doesn't mean you're cheap."

Another short gasp. "You think I'm beautiful?"

"Don't do that," I warn, actually lifting the phone to my ear. "Don't get that excited tone in your voice."

"There's no excitement in my tone."

"Jules, you're beautiful, you're intelligent, and you're the woman of my dreams. I want to have mind-blowing, intimate sex with you," I whisper. Then I snicker when her car swerves, knowing my words struck a nerve and threw her off kilter.

I can almost feel the warmth in her blushing cheeks and see her smile through the receiver. I wasn't lying—she *is* beautiful. She has these kind-hearted blue eyes that smile all on their own, without instruction. Her wild, crazy blond curls bounce when she walks, and gently sway when she's still. Her hair actually reminds me of the sun, the way the room lights up when those curls walk in. Her cheeks are high, her ass looks great in a pair of jeans, and she doesn't overdo the makeup. Not to mention, she has a handful up top that any man would be lucky to hold.

When it comes to physical traits, on a scale of one to ten, Jules Stone is a solid fifty.  It's no surprise that guys are instantly attracted to her in the first place—she's hot as hell. I'm disappointed that she's so sensitive and a little crazy, too. If she weren't, I'm pretty sure more guys might have been interested in taking her out, instead of just wanting to bang her.

"What else should I know?" She wonders out loud, but I'm not quite sold on the fact that she's speaking to me. "What would make a guy want to stay with me?"

I sigh, a bit annoyed with how needy she sounds. "Why do you need a guy in the first place?"

"A girl spends her whole life wanting to be in love. I grew up with these ideas, and I see others having what I wish I had. A hand to hold, a shoulder to cry on, a prince to save me. I just want to be saved. I want to be somebody's princess."

I know this is Disney's fault. "Can I be frank with you?" I ask but don't wait for her reply. "There's no castle. There's no one galloping in on a white horse. There's no prince who's going to show up and save you. What you need to do is save yourself."

"How do I do that?"

"Simple. You realize you don't need saving."

"Ugh. It must be *so* easy being a guy, never falling head over heels, never putting down your shield of protection from heartbreak."

I chuckle at her comment, noticing that it's all too wrong. "We fall and have heartbreaks, too. We just don't spend the next few years reliving those days on repeat wondering what we could have done differently. We simply get drunk, have meaningless sex, and move on."

"Ha! See that's the problem! When you guys are having meaningless sex, we girls are having *hopeful* sex! Hoping for a second date, a second call, and a second everything. You guys are making us hopefuls meaningless."

"Which takes us back to rule number one—don't sleep with us because we call you beautiful."

I can almost see her smile through the cell phone. "Touché."

"All right, Jules. I'm gonna hang up. The snow's coming down faster, and I would feel more comfortable getting you to your personal hell in one piece."

"Okay, but Kayden?" Her voice jumps an octave in a question mark and I wait for her thoughts. "Thank you. For doing this."

Before I can reply, she hangs up. I look at the back of her head in the driver's seat in the car in front of me and I let a sigh move though my lungs. She's tousling her hair around, running her fingers through the locks, and for a second I want to be running my hands through it, finding the gentle spots behind her ear, licking her body from the tip of her toes to the curve of her neck. She's weird as fuck, but I bet she can transform that weirdness into some awesome sex moves…

The bulge forming in my jeans snaps me back to reality. Wait, what?! *Stop.* What in the goddamn hell am I talking about? *Bad, Kayden, bad!* I can't have these types of thoughts about Jules. I can't want to push her against the hood of the car and press into her, forcing moans to escape closed lips. I can't allow the melting snow to run down her body as I wipe up each wet spot with my tongue. This is business and mixing business with pleasure is bad form...Right?

*I will not bang my boss. I will not bang my boss.*

Ah hell. I still want to bang my boss.

We pull our cars over to fill up on gas, and all I can from the pump behind her is stare at her perfect ass. The way she handles the pump is way too much of a turn on for me, which is awkward, so I force my eyes to shift away from her.

"I'll cover your ass, too," she says, looking toward me with those eyes. I blink through the snowflakes hitting my eyelashes and try to understand what the hell she just said. She sees my confusion and smiles, speaking louder. "I said I'll cover your gas. Just let me know how much it is."

"Don't worry about it."

Snow falls down her jacket and into her cleavage and my eyes follow it. It's probably melting now, leaving dripping wet water rolling down her body. *Jesus!*

"I'm gonna head inside. Do you want my lips?" she asks, raising an eyebrow. My weird expression is probably freaking her out. She laughs, and the way her head throws backwards is so fucking attractive. "My gosh, you're like the people in the nursing home where I volunteer! Put in your hearing aids, oldie. I said, *Do-you-want-some-chips*?"

"Oh…no. I'm good. I'll be in my car, ready to follow when you come out."

I watch her move quickly into the gas station and slap my hand against my forehead. "What the hell, Kayden?"

Hopping in my car, I slam the door and grip the steering wheel. "Pull it together…"

Reaching for my ashtray, I pick up a cigarette and light it, waiting for Jules to come back out and finish off the road trip. The snow's coming down faster and faster, and we have quite a few more hours left before hitting her cabin.

Seeing her walk back to her car and hop in, I turn my engine on and wait for her to pull out. What follows next is the sound of her car trying to get a move on but failing terribly. Then I see her body jump, as a cloud of smoke appears from under the hood. She starts thrashing her arms around, slapping her hands against the steering wheel, screaming what I assume to be pretty harsh cuss words.

Opening my door, I walk over and she rolls down her window by hand in her old-ass car. Placing my hands on the door, I bend down to see her frowning. What a cute frown it is though.

"This is turning out to be the crappiest day of the year," she sighs and lets her head fall back to the steering wheel.

"Don't be crazy. There's no way this is the crappiest day of the year," I say, nudging her in the shoulder through her car window. "There's always Christmas to look forward to."

"You don't happen to know anything about cars?" she asks, glancing at the time and groaning in exasperation. It's difficult for me to understand why she's in such a hurry to arrive at a place she calls her personal hell, but then again, she's pretty damn weird.

"Nope, not a mechanic. But with my superb talent I *can* play one on television."

She smiles, making me smile. Her smile is killing me. Her gray mittens run across her hair and her body rotates to me. "Listen, I know you've been clean from killing people for a week now, and I would hate for you to slip up and have an incident but…do you think I can bum a ride? If you end up killing me, that's totally understandable, and I apologize ahead of time for making you relapse." She looks at me, removing her mittens, and I notice two small dimples on her cheeks as her fingers brush through her hair.

I watch her roll her window back up before I open her door and take her hand, helping her out of the broken-down vehicle. Moving over to the passenger side of my car, I open the door and she climbs in. After I head inside to get the dude who works at the gas station to help me push Jules's car into an emptied parking spot until the holiday weekend is over, I move to hop back into the BMW.

"What about my bags?!" she exclaims in her overly dramatic way, a trait I picked up on the first moment I met her.

"Keys," I order, and she hands them to me. Loading her luggage into my trunk, I hurry to get out of the frigid air and brush off the freshly fallen snow that covers me. Slamming my door shut, I sigh. "Your bags really made it hard for the body in my trunk to fit."

She smiles again. I don't know why, but it pleases me that I make her smile. I want to keep those grins coming my way.

"Is it a girl body or a guy body?"

"Guy, of course. He stiffed me at bar close on my tips. Besides"—I start up my engine and pull out of the gas station—"there are a lot of things I would do to a girl's body. But I would never hurt her."

She arches an eyebrow, looking at me as if she hasn't seen me until now. Holy shit, I want to kiss her. She once again runs her hands through her hair, her eyes glued to me. She's still for a good minute until she turns to the GPS and enters her family's address.

"Smoking kills."

"So do airplanes, ovens, and peanut butter."

She rolls her eyes and runs her hands up and down her thighs. I would kill to be her hands right now. "Yeah, but those are accidents. Smoking those cancer sticks is a choice."

"Does it bother you?"

"Oh no. Not at all. It's just been proven in studies that second-hand smoke can affect people just as terribly as first-hand smoking. I'm fine with breathing in your toxins, shortening my life expectancy by minutes…hours…days…"

I narrow my eyes on her and blow out a cloud of smoke toward the open crack in my window. "Well, as long as it doesn't bother you."

"You're such a dick. I don't even know you but I can tell you're a total dick."

I chuckle, smashing my cigarette into the ashtray. "You're not a very nice made-up girlfriend." She smiles at the ashtray, pleased with my choice to respect her hope for longevity.

"I know. I'm a total girl-dick. That's why we work so well as a make-believe couple. We're terrible people and putting us together pretty much makes us the devil." Her eyes sparkle almost more than the snow outside and her lips part again. "I know this is going to sound inappropriate, random and stuff, but…you're pretty hot." Her comment comes as a surprise, and I smirk as the color rises up her cheeks. "I even made up a nickname for you."

"A nickname, eh? Let me hear it."

"Promise you won't laugh?" she asks sounding a bit nervous.

"I'll probably laugh."

She wiggles her nose and bites her bottom lip, "Mr. Sexdorable."

I laugh instantly. How could I not? "Sexdorable?"

"You know, 'cause you're sexy and adorable all at once."

I relax into my seat and can't stop laughing, "Guys don't like being called adorable. Puppies are adorable, not grown men."

"Even if it's *sex*dorable?" she pouts, hoping I will agree to the name.

"Well…" I ponder the thought, rubbing my hand across my chin. "Since I'm getting paid one thousand dollars to act like your boyfriend, I think I'll let the nickname slide for now."

She laughs this time and I feel a knot in my gut. My gawd…I love the sound of her laugh, too. Almost more than those smiles.

"What about me? Do I get a nickname?" She slips her feet out of her wet boots. Her frame rotates toward me and she curls her body up in her seat, tucking her knees against her chest. If it were anyone else, I would cuss them out for having their feet on my BMW seats, but her socks have penguins on them, and that's pretty damn cute.

"Sunshine."

Her smile widens, her dimples deepen, and I think about holding her. This time the thought of having sex with her doesn't even appear.

"Sunshine?" she questions, moving her hair behind her ears. "There's this old guy at the nursing home where I volunteer and he calls me Sunshine."

"He sounds like a smart guy," I say and she giggles.

"He's kind of an asshole, who's snarky and rude. But I like him well enough. So tell me, why the nickname 'Sunshine?'"

"Because even during some dark times in your life, when the clouds roll in, you still find a way to laugh, to shine." She's still again, but that's perfect. I don't want her to move. I know it might sound stupid, but if she never moved again and just kept smiling, I would be a happy man.

I pause, realizing my thoughts, and shake my head back and forth. Where the heck did that come from? First I want to bang her, and now I want to stare at her? All of her awkwardness is shifting into me and I need to pull it together.

Hell. This isn't real. This isn't real.

*Think dirty thoughts again, Kayden. I want to bang my boss, I want to bang my boss, I want to hold her hand...*

I glance over at her, feeling her body shift in her seat. "Oh..." she whispers, and I look down to see that her hand has somehow intertwined with mine. "Is this so it doesn't appear awkward when we get to my parents?"

*No, I just like holding your hand.* "Yeah. You know, we want this to be believable."

"Right. Well, Kayden, I gotta say...I almost feel as though you like me...and we've only known each other a few hours. You deserve a damn Oscar." She bites that damn lip again, and I just about lose it. She's a wacko, she's funny, she's exaggeratedly emotional, and she's holding my hand.

And the last thing I want her to do is let go.

"You can't go a little faster?" Jules complains, and I choose not to reply. We are a good two hours behind schedule, and with this timeline, we should be to her house a little after nine p.m. Jules's head falls into her hands and she mutters against her palms, "There aren't even that many cars on the road!"

"Don't get bitchy," I warn, not looking her way. "We'll get there when we get there. What's the big deal anyway?"

Her cell phone goes off for the fifth time in the past hour and she stares at it before holding the shining phone up to my face. "*That's* the big deal. My mother's a nut and won't stop calling. I've texted her three times already telling her we were running behind. And now she's calling nonstop."

"Maybe that's not why she's calling. Just answer it. You're acting like a little brat."

She straightens up in her seat and gives me a look of death. "You cannot call me a brat!"

The phone relentlessly rings again demanding an answer. Just as defiantly, Jules ignores it, again. "Brat. Brat…*Brat*!" I echo her way. Her middle finger flies up toward me but cute smirk on her face remains. I bite toward her finger, which isn't giving me the kindest gesture in the world. “If you point that at me, I will bite it. Hard. Now answer the damn phone.”

She laughs at me, watching me snap my teeth toward her before a flat sigh leaves her body and she answers her cell phone. “Hi Mom.” Jules melts into the leather seat and nods as if her mother can see her actions. “I know, but there’s—” She pauses, listening to her mom, who is not giving her a chance to get a word in. “Yeah, but Mom!” Her childish whiney voice returns and I snicker. I can’t help but think that we have pretty different mothers.

“Of course he’s here! Where the heck would he be? *Noo,* I’m not lying.” Pause. Frown. Pause. Frown again. “Well I don’t really care what Lisa thinks. No, he’s not a Republican! My gosh, Mom!”

The phone rips away from her ear and she turns toward me. “Are you a Republican?”

“No.”

Her ear flies back to the phone and her intense look of displeasure returns. “Mom, if you think I’m going to ask him that, you’re ridiculous. Why not? Are you serious?! Because it’s totally inappropriate. I’m a grown woman who is completely capable of choosing my boyfriends, Mother! And I refuse to sit here and listen to you—” Her words come to a halt and the eye rolling hits an all-time high. She covers the phone with her hand and pushes it in my direction. "She wants to talk to you."

I laugh and shake my head back and forth. "I'm driving."

"Listen. I'm trying here, I really am. But if I have to sit and listen to how childish I am for not giving my boyfriend the phone when my mom asked to speak with him, I will promise to make the next five days of your life a living hell." The phone pushes more into my arm and I really want to laugh at her, but she's kind of scary right now. "Remember, you're Richard."

Grabbing the phone, I place it against my ear. "Hello?"

A woman's warm velvet voice sweetly responds. "Oh! Hello, Richard! I'm Jules's mother, Tina. I just wanted to say hi before meeting in a few hours. I'm sorry you both are running behind. I told Julie Anne to leave earlier, but you know how hardheaded she can be."

I smirk, because I have a good idea about how stubborn Jules can be. I wonder where she picked up those traits? "Yeah, well, it's my fault. I had to work a little later than planned. But we should be there sooner than later."

"Perfect. So, we'll make for a late dinner. Which is fine. I'll see you both soon. All right? Oh! And Richard?" Without waiting for my acknowledgment, she immediately continues, "Jules has a history of picking guys who end up liking her for certain reasons. You sound different, though. I just hope you're okay with who we are and don't find it to be too much of a…shock. We're down to earth like all the rest."

Before I can respond to her weird comment, Tina hangs up and I hand the phone back to Jules. "What did she mean by 'our family's down to earth like the rest'? Who says that?" I see her body physically tighten up. Her blue eyes turn away from me and face the window, where she proceeds to give me the cold shoulder. It's something she doesn't want to talk about, and now I want to know even more, but I don't push the matter. If she wanted me to know, she would have told me, right? Besides, all of her family's secrets aren't my business; I am only her boyfriend for the next few days anyway.

After a while, her hand finds mine again, and for the rest of the ride we're quiet, just holding on to each other, traveling through the snow. As we round the corner to this gigantic cabin, I get a bit confused. "This isn't a cabin, Jules! It's a mansion made out of wood!" I feel Jules's fingers tighten around mine from the idea of entering. She doesn't respond to my comment because she seems too nervous to operate. "Hey, you're fine."

"I'm fine…" she mutters, holding on even tighter. "I'm fine."

Her eyes start to tear up, and I see the crying girl from earlier creeping in. "Oh come on, Sunshine. Don't give away your power to people who don't deserve it. You may not be able to control the weather—or the family you're born into—but you can control who you allow to hurt you, who you allow to affect you."

"How do you change a lifetime or being the black sheep of the family who is always crying?"

"Well, for starters you find a moment when you would usually cry and you choose not to. You change direction and hold your head up high. And you say, 'Fuck you, motherfuckers! I'm Jules Stone and I'm motherfucking awesome!'"

She laughs out loud, and I swear to God she snorts. She snorts, and I realize I've never seen something so damn adorable in my whole life. Sexdorable, even. Jules Stone is pretty damn sexdorable.

"Come on," I challenge, nudging my hand against her knee. "Say it."

"Kayden, no." She keeps laughing, and I keep falling.

"Please?" I whisper, taking my hand and rubbing the back of her neck. Every time I touch her, it feels as if we have been touching for years. I don't know how, and I don't know why, but when I touch this girl, I feel at home.

"My name is Jules Stone and I'm motherfucking awesome!"

Pulling up toward the home, I see two Audi and one Mercedes in the driveway, and the first thing I think is, *Why the hell is Jules driving that broken-down Honda?* Before we have time to even put the car in park, the front door is opening and people are gathering on the porch.

"I'm fine, I'm fine…I'm…" she mutters, her words fading off, so I finish for her.

"Fine." I smile and she smiles back. "We're fine."

She wiggles her nose once and goes to open her door but pauses. "Oh! A heads-up, I think we're in love." She freezes, cursing under her breath, and slaps her hand against her face. "I mean, *you* as in *Richard*. Richard and I are in love."

"Right. I love you." The words roll off my tongue and it scares me how much it doesn't scare me. "Don't open your door. Let me do it for you, ya know, since we are so deeply in love and stuff."

She sits back in her seat and nods once. I jump out of the car and play the role of an awesome boyfriend by pulling open her door and helping her out of the car.

When she stands inches below me, I go in for the extra one-two punch and kiss her forehead. Wrapping her against my body I whisper one more time as we begin walking toward the awaiting party, "We're fine."

The way she snuggles into me makes me think that she actually believes me—which, in turn, secretly makes my night complete. The closer we get to the front of the cabin, the slower I begin to walk until my jaw drops to the ground and I stand frozen in place. Twisting my body toward Jules, I yank her to the side.

"Holy shit! Is that Lisa Stone?! And Danny Everson?! And holy shit—that's Matt and Tina Stone! Holy fuck, you're Jules Stone!" The realization sets in as I come to terms with the fact that Jules' family is *THE* Stone family—one of Hollywood's most celebrated families for their crazy amount of work on the big screen. And Danny Everson is known for his Oscars and insane films.

I shoot the words to Jules and watch her stumble back, saddened that she couldn't keep the fact hidden. Then I watch her lips turn down. She's disappointed by my realization. "Yes…*Richard.*" She scolds me with her tone, and I realize how fast I almost blew my cover.

"Right. I'm sorry. But geez…You didn't think that was something you could have mentioned in the past five hours?!"

"It slipped my mind." She moves toward her house, leaving me a bit stunned. It slipped her mind? I'm supposing to act through this weekend with Oscar-winning performers?

Yeah freakin' right.

"Finally! Did you give him the wrong address or something, Julie Anne?" were the first words from her mother as she pulls her into a hug.

"No, it just so happens there's a snow storm, Mom. No big deal." Jules turns toward me and holds her hand out in my direction, which I take, because screw it, I'm a professional.

"Mom, Dad"—her eyes roll as she mumbles, not looking toward Danny or Lisa—"everyone else, this is Richard."

I extend my hand and shake hands with Oscar winners. Jesus. My life just went to a pretty good place. "Nice to meet you all," I say, and mean, more than any words I have ever spoken.

Jules's dad, *the* Matt Stone, pats me on the back and pulls me toward the house. "You hungry, Rich? I can call you Rich, yes?"

"Sir, you can call me anything you want." I smirk as I follow him inside. He could call me asswipe and I would be flattered. I listen to Jules talking to her mom—or well, getting scolded by her mom for not greeting her sister and Danny.

"Do you have to be so childish, Julie Anne?" Tina hisses, moving everyone into the living room.

"Sorry. Hi Lisa. Danny." I watch Jules roll her eyes and can't help but laugh at her stubbornness.

"Hey Jules," Danny smiles and goes in for an awkward hug, and for some reason, the amount of time he holds on to her annoys me. "You lose weight?"

"Gained ten pounds," Jules says, but I doubt it's true. I couldn't imagine her ten pounds lighter than she is now; she has perfect curves to her.

"Oh…it looks good on you."

Awkward silence. I'm still looking at Jules's curves, and I'm getting pissed because so is Danny. "Should we grab our luggage now?" I ask, changing the subject from the weird vibe happening. It's nice to see another dysfunctional family. It brings me a bit of comfort.

"No, don't worry about it. Danny and I will grab it after dinner for you. You're our guest!" Matt pats me on the back again, and I can't help but feel star-struck every time this guy talks my way.

"Where's Grandma?" Jules asks her mother.

"Oh, she couldn't make it. She said that she and the new *boyfriend* are skiing in the Alps for the holiday." The way Tina says the word *boyfriend* has a sting to it. I'm not sure if anyone else picks up on it, but the sound of Tina's disapproval of her mother's new guy is pretty damn clear.

"What?! Grandma's the whole reason I said I would come!" Jules is pouting again, so I walk over and wrap my arms around her from behind and kiss her cheek, feeling her relax into me.

Out of nowhere a little girl streaks through the cabin completely naked. She couldn't have been any older than three or four. I help Jules remove her jacket as she chuckles at her young niece running around in her birthday suit. "Don't mind Olivia. She's always naked." The sweet tone in her voice takes on an edge when she adds, "just like her mother." Another passive aggressive comment from one of the Stone family members. I make a mental note to brace myself against these snide comments and not-so-subtle potshots that this family takes at one another with such malicious ease.

Lisa tries to brush off Jules' rude comment even as the blush of embarrassment reddens her face. I can't even lie—Lisa is also beautiful. She's pretty skinny, but not stick-thin. Her long brown hair moves perfectly with her, and her deep blue eyes match her mother's. She and Jules are about the same height, but if I didn't know they were related, I would never have considered it to be true. They are opposites in almost every way. Jules has these adorable blue doe eyes, and Lisa possesses the intense, cat-shaped, sexed-up eyes that always appear in her movies.

There's an uncomfortable silence filling the room, so I try my best to defuse it. "She's beautiful," I say, gesturing—but not looking—at the naked girl running around the space.

Danny laughs. "You don't have to be nice. She looks like an alien."

Stunned by his rude comment, I hardly know what to say. "I beg your pardon?"

"An alien," Tina reinforces about her granddaughter. "It's not an insult. Aliens are really the big thing in Hollywood right now. That's what's hot in the industry."

"If we get her started before she's four, she'll be golden." Danny chimes in.

"I think horror movies are going to be her money maker, you know, with the creepy kid look and stuff," Lisa adds.

The three of them laugh and that's when I see it, that's when I notice everything that makes Jules her awkward, crying self. She came from a house of nut job Hollywood weirdos. They just called that sweet, innocent, beautiful little girl a creepy looking alien. What. The. Fuck?!

Matt, Jules's father, is the only one who doesn't join in on the bullying. He reaches for the naked girl and lifts her into his arms. "Don't listen to them, Olivia. You're a perfect princess. Now, let's go get you into some pajamas and ready for dinner." The little girl smiles to her grandfather and wraps her arms around his neck.

Leaning in toward Jules, I whisper against her ear, "Are they always like this?"

"You haven't even experienced the true blue Stone family dinner yet."

"Here, let me put your coats in your bedroom," Danny offers, reaching for Jules' jacket, and I toss mine off to him before watching him disappear down the hallway.

"Let me make you a drink?" I ask Jules, nodding my head toward the bar in the other room.

She turns and stares into my eyes. A smile creeps on her lips and the overwhelmed look she's worn since we pulled into the driveway is slowly fading. "Make it a strong one."

"Always." Releasing her, I move toward the bar and start preparing her some fruity girl drink, because I'm almost positive that's something she would love. Then I pull out another glass to get me some whiskey, hoping for a somewhat easy dinner and then bed. Out of nowhere, Jules's sister Lisa appears and takes a seat at the bar, leaning forward.

I'm not a dumbass, so I know the leaning is to give me a clear shot down at her fake tits, but I only look into her eyes. "Can I get ya something?"

"I'll just take this," she says as she grabs Jules's drink and starts to suck it down. "So…you're Julie's boyfriend, eh? I'm Lisa, the wicked sister."

"Richard." I extend my hand toward her, giving her my fake name, and she accepts, "Nice to meet you. I actually saw your latest film, *The Forbidden Gatekeepers*, a few weeks ago. Amazing work."

"Well thank you. We filmed that a few years back, and it was nice to finally get it to the big screen." She runs her fingers through her hair and leans back on her seat. "I have another fantasy film coming out in a few months. You should convince Jules to bring you to the premiere in Hollywood. I would ask her, but…"

She doesn't finish her thought because it's pretty much a useless comment. She knows Jules wouldn't want to go, and I can completely understand. If there's anything I understand, it's sibling issues. "I'll ask her."

"No. Never mind. Stupid for me to even bring it up." She edges around in her chair, making herself more comfortable, and changes the direction of the conversation. "So how did Jules and you meet?"

I shift my eyes back to Jules, realizing we never talked about how we met. Well, time to make up some bullshit. "A bar." Easy enough—people meet at bars all the time. Lisa crumples up her nose and I can't help but notice. "What's wrong?"

"Jules hates bars. I think her boyfriend before you broke up with her in a bar. It's just funny that you two met at one."

"Oh yeah, well. She was out celebrating her friend's promotion or something. Anyway, I ordered her drinks, but she refused them. It wasn't until bar close that she allowed me to exchange numbers with her. Then from there, we took off."

"How long have you been together?"

"Seven months. Which doesn't seem like a long time, but"—I chuckle, turning in Jules' direction to see her engaged in a conversation with her mom—"if you know Jules, it takes less than an hour to figure her out. And I'm crazy about what I've figured out so far." That's the genuine truth.

"Hmm…" Lisa hums, appearing in deep thought. "Did she ever mention us to you? Like who we are?"

"Nope. Needless to say, I was a bit taken aback walking into the cabin to find Oscars and Golden Globes awards hanging around on bookshelves."

Reaching across to me, she places her hand on my forearm, and bends forward. "No need to make a big deal about it. We're just like the rest of the world. Only we poop out gold." She winks, and I'm offended. She's flirting with me, and I say a little prayer, hoping the rest of the weekend doesn't involve her flirtation. It goes without saying that, from working in a bar, I've met a lot of Lisa Stone types. They think they are top shelf due to their looks, their sex appeal. But there's nothing sexy about it. Plus, they normally turn out to be shitty in bed. The ones who surprise the hell out of me in the bedroom are the quirky ones, the shy ones, and the ones who embarrass easily. They always bring their A game. Lisa Stone is probably a solid D+ under the sheets. But Jules? Let's just say I still want to bang my boss.

"It's funny. Jules never said how good-looking you are. It would definitely be something she would've mentioned, too. Jules is always trying to outdo me." I don't reply, mainly because her comment is out of left field, awkward, and uncomfortable. "I remember when I auditioned for my first movie. I was eleven, and Jules was twelve. After I landed the part, she showed up with straight As. Just to downplay my success."

"Maybe she wanted to be noticed, too."

"No, she did it to be spiteful."

I laugh at the idea of a twelve-year-old being spiteful. "She was a kid."

Lisa stares into me, and her eyes are not anything like her sister's gentle eyes. Lisa's eyes are completely devoid of the sweetness and sensitivity in Jules' eyes. Her lips part as she whispers, "It was my first movie. I could have had that moment." She takes another sip of her drink and smiles. "Wow, this is delish. Do you think you can drop a cherry into it?" She leans in closer, and I see the pink lace on her bra fighting its way out of her shirt. I look under the cabinet and see a fresh jar of cherries, and then I look up and see Jules staring at me from the living room, a frown on her lips. When her eyes meet mine, I mouth the words, "You all right?" toward her and she nods, mouthing the same question to me. My left shoulder rises and falls and I see her chuckle a small bit before she turns back to her mom.

Returning my attention to Lisa, I reply to her question. "Sorry, looks like we're fresh out of cherries." I start moving toward Jules to give her my whiskey. She will definitely need something stronger than a fruity drink to make it through this evening. After I hand her the drink, her mom wanders off to make sure everything is ready for dinner.

"Kayden what's wrong? Is everything okay?" Jules asks. The expression of extreme anxiety on my face is probably freaking her out.

I run my hands over my face, knowing that if this situation was reversed, I would hope that Jules would be upfront with me. "Yeah, everything's fine. It's just…" I take a deep breath, hoping that I don't send Jules into overdrive with anger. "Lisa was just hitting on me."

Her hand flies to her chest and the look of worry overtaking her eyes is sad as hell. "What? What did she do? Are you sure?"

"Yeah, I'm sure. She was leaning up close to make sure I could see down her blouse. Plus she kept touching my arm and flipping her hair." A small chuckle escapes Jules's lips and she covers her mouth to try to spare my ego from her following fit of giggles. I shift my body, crossing my arms. "I'm sorry. This is…funny?"

Yup, she's still giggling. "She wasn't hitting on you."

I narrow my eyes and nod slowly. "Yes, she was, Jules. Look I know this might be tough with the whole Danny-Lisa situation but she was…"

"Did she kiss you?"

Her question is abrupt, which leads to me fumbling my words. "Wh—what? No of course not."

"Sorry, hun. She wasn't flirting with you."

"I think I know what flirting looks like, Jules. I've had tons of women hit on me!"

"Wow, no low self esteem here, eh? Really? *Tons*?" She snickers again, and her father walks over to join us, asking Jules what's so funny. "Oh nothing. My boyfriend thinks Lisa was flirting with him."

Matt's eyes widen as he turns to me. "She kissed you?!"

"What?! No. But…" I'm feeling more and more uncomfortable as I start self-doubting my interaction with Lisa. Was she hitting on me? Am I overthinking it? I clear my throat, ready to explain. "There was winking. She also mentioned how good looking I was and stuff."

"So…?" Matt glares at me, waiting for the real true-blue juicy details—which I don't have. But hell! She was flirting with me! Matt sighs, patting me on the back. "Rich, you *are* a good looking guy. But, Lisa doesn't flirt. She makes out. And the winking thing? Well, she had a weird spa facial procedure with her mother a few years back. Now she just winks randomly. Best not to bring it up in a conversation—she's super self-conscious about it."

My shoulders slump down, and reality sets in. Turning toward Jules, I see a sweet smile resting on her face. "So…she wasn't hitting on me?"

Moving over to me, she shrugs. "Better luck next time. Come on, dinner's ready." She and her dad start toward the dining room, leaving me standing there with a heavy level of bewilderment.

Well shit.

That's embarrassing.

# 4 Jules

## *My Boyfriend's Nuts*

I can't believe I'm sitting at this dining room table, about to eat dinner with my family and fake boyfriend. Kayden looks fantastic. Then again, he hasn't stopped looking fantastic since I met him. I just want to snuggle into his neck and make believe forever.

When the thought fills my head, I shake it back and forth. Kayden warned me about this—the way I fall for any guy who looks at me. Which is sad, but true. After the Danny heartbreak, I figured I wasn't good enough for anyone. Therefore, I settled for everyone. But since I met Kayden…seven hours ago…I'm a new woman! No more one-night stands! No more changing myself to make guys interested.

I'm going to be me, and if they don't like that, well, screw them. I'm Jules Stone and I'm motherfucking awesome!

My eyes shift over to Kayden again, and I sigh. I still want to snuggle into him and make believe forever…which is sad because I know this is nothing more than an act.

"So Richard, Jules says you're into accounting?" Dad asks, and I instantly feel bad. Kayden is too beautiful to be called a Richard.

"Yeah, but I'm thinking of diving into the business world. I'm really interested in commercial marketing."

"Oh yeah? Did you go to school for that?"

"Actually I took a few classes, hoping to re-enroll in a few months. You know what they say. 'It's never too late to start over.'" I about lose it when I see Kayden's full-toothed grin, directed at Dad. It's the most charming smile I've seen in all of my life, and I want it to never disappear.

"You ever think about acting?" Danny asks, and I hate him for interacting with Kayden. I also hate him because he looks good, handsome even. It looks like he's been working out; he's looking really buff. And tan, too. He's probably preparing for another movie role. Why does he have to look so good? I hate myself for thinking how good he looks, and I hate myself even more for wishing I were wearing my push-up bra.

"I beg your pardon?" Kayden asks, a bit thrown off by Danny's question. I'll admit that I am, too.

Danny laughs as he picks at his salad. I always hated that about him—how he picks at his food. *Just eat it already!* "I ask because, well, you're a good-looking guy."

His hands fly up and he laughs again. What a stupid laugh. "No offense, Jules. I'm not hitting on your boyfriend."

"Why not? It wouldn't be the first time you hit on something that should have been off limits." Even as the words roll off my tongue I taste it—my bitter resentment. Yup. It's been over five years and I'm still replaying the memories, the scars through my head every single day. But how can I not? *She's my sister.*

"Jules, that was unnecessary," Dad scolds me. Mom chimes in quickly, pointing out the inappropriateness of my behavior, especially in front of a guest…my guest, the fake boyfriend. When I look over to Kayden, I feel like a complete fool and mutter an apology, but he shakes his head, refusing to accept it, and squeezes my knee under the table.

He clears his throat and that deep, smoky voice reappears. "Why do you ask, Danny?" The awkward bomb that's destined to explode sometime over these next few days is defused for the time being by Kayden and his charm.

"Oh, well, I'm currently in the works of auditioning for a movie and could use someone to run lines with. I would ask Matt, but he embarrasses me by how freaking amazing he is. Plus, he rehearses in the nude. But mostly, I'm intimated by his talent."

Dad laughs and rolls his eyes at Danny, smitten by his comment. I wish Dad would act like he despised Danny a little whenever I was around. Would that be too much to ask for?

Kayden looks at me, wondering how he should respond to Danny's invite, hoping not to betray me; but, I nod to give him the OK. Who knew? Maybe it could help Kayden with his acting career.

"I would help; but…" Kayden nuzzles my neck, planting a light kiss there. "I'm really focused on connecting with Jules these next few days, to see where she comes from." Kayden's words are so caring and thoughtful, and I feel the knots in my stomach tighten a bit more. He has to know that running lines with someone like Danny could lead to some amazing networking, but he chooses against it, picking me over his career.

Not to sound super annoying and pathetic; but hell, I'm going to sound super annoying and pathetic because that's what I do best—no one has ever put me first. It feels pretty freaking good to be chosen first.

A chef enters with homemade, super fancy gourmet pizzas. The table slowly starts to fill up with more and more options, and as the food keeps coming out, my stomach starts growling.

Everyone starts to dive into the food, and Mom can't help but apologize to Kayden for the 'lame' dinner spread. "We decided on an easier meal for tonight, saving the more elaborate meals for the next few days. I hope you like pizza."

"It just so happens pizza is my favorite food of all time. So I think we're off to a good start."Avoiding all the fancy over-the-top pizzas, Kayden reaches for the pepperoni. The only reason there is a pepperoni pizza on the table is because of me. I hate all of the garbage people toss onto pizzas. Keep it clean and simple. Dad calls me a picky eater; I call him a Hollywood eater.

"Good, I'm glad. So, Jules told me about how you both met, and I find it amazingly romantic," Mom says to Kayden, sliding a slice of pizza onto her plate.

"Really? It didn't sound that romantic at all to me. But I guess that's because Richard over here told the story. Guys always leave out the romance," Lisa says, and I arch an eyebrow in Kayden's direction. He told her how we met? But how? I told Mom how we met! And I doubt his story involved the horses and white roses! Plus, I'm really beginning to hate the way people are calling him Richard.

Kayden smiles and laughs to himself. "Well, you know us guys…We're idiots like that." He edges closer to me and pretends to kiss my neck as he whispers, "How did we meet? I said in a bar."

When he pulls away, I slowly shake my head back and forth. This is discomforting. Reaching for the glass of wine in front of me, I grab and chug. And chug…and chug some more.

Mom laughs. "Lisa, you never did get a hold of the romance bug. I think it was sweet! The way he hired a horse and carriage in the park just to get her attention."

And let the choking on wine begin. Only this time, it isn't me choking; it's my fake boyfriend, who is the best actor ever. The way his face is turning red and the veins in his neck are popping out is super convincing. Distraction is the key with this family, but this, well…it seems a bit extreme.

"Water…" he mutters, and I am just about ready to give him an Oscar from the bookshelf until he reaches for the glass of water and knocks it over. "Nuts…" he chokes out, patting his neck before pushing away from the table.

Nuts?!

Oh my gosh. He's allergic to nuts.

"Mom! Are there nuts in the tomato sauce?" Choking on my own panic, I watch Kayden struggle as I feel my own throat tightening. As he fights for every breath, my breathing becomes labored with his.

Mom's eyes register extreme concern, along with Dad's anxious blue eyes. "Um, I think—in the sauce. Pecans, I think." I see her face shift to anger, and that anger is now directed toward me. "You told me he wasn't allergic to anything! I called and asked!"

Kayden continues scratching at his itching neck as he clears his throat. "No, it's fine."

"I *asked* you, Jules!" Mom yells again, making me feel as if I'm the worst person in the world.

I sigh, willing myself to become invisible. I turn when I hear Kayden coughing, worry filling me up. "You're breaking out," I whimper, seeing his neck turn red just from a few bites of the pizza.

Dad pushes his chair away from the table in a hurry. "Do you need to go to the hospital?"

Kayden shakes his head back and forth. "I'll be fine." He sips at my water on the table and continues to cough.

Standing from his seat, Dad moves toward the kitchen. "I'll grab some allergy pills." And he's gone. Mom's still fuming; I can almost see the smoke blowing from her ears.

"Julie Anne, I asked you!"

"No, it's my fault," Kayden coughs and tries to smile. "I probably confused her and…" He's choking on his words and stands from the table. "Excuse me really fast."

He hurries out of the room, toward the bathroom, and everything blurs as tears fill my eyes. I look up and see Danny smirking. I pull my napkin off my lap and toss it on the table.

"Yeah, Daniel, keep laughing, because a person having an allergic reaction is funny." Running in Kayden's direction, I sigh and knock on the bathroom door. Dad sees me and hands me a glass of water and allergy pills, which I thank him for as I continue to knock.

Opening the door, he grins as he's holds a wet cloth around his neck. "I'm so sorry, Sunshine. I should be good in a few. I'm sorry. Shit!" he mutters under his breath, and I step into the bathroom closing the door behind me, locking us inside. He's pissed at himself for eating something that's deadly to him. I know it's awful, and I know I'm probably going to hell…but I find him extremely sexy right now. Pushing the glass of water toward him, I place the pills in the palm of his hand and he downs them quickly.

Gesturing to the toilet seat, I order him to sit down and he tells me he's all right. "Please, Kay?" I beg, and he narrows his somewhat puffy eyes on me, and sits. Taking the cloth from his hands, I kneel in from of him and start holding it against his neck.

"I should've asked," I say, feeling awful.

"Yeah, you should have. You're a terrible, heartless person," he laughs, closing his eyes. "So what happened exactly? With the whole Danny-and-Lisa situation?"

I sit back on my heels and rest my hands in my lap as he opens his eyes and finds my stare. "It's a long story."

"I have time."

Wiggling my nose, I debate running away, avoiding speaking the memories out loud. But the way he takes my hands and holds them, even when people aren't watching, makes me feel as if it's not only information that he wants to know for character study. It seems as if he simply wants to know about me.

"We dated for three years. And well, as you know, for Danny being a Hollywood god, that's a pretty long relationship. I loved him. Even though he only semi-liked me. When I told him I was thinking of giving up on the acting thing after not instantly breaking into the industry like Lisa, well…" My eyes shift to the floor, reliving the moment that changed everything.

"He never told me he wasn't okay with it. He always put on a smile and kissed me like he meant it. But then again, he's Danny Everson, one of the best actors out there. And right around that time, he was just hitting it big. Then, for Easter, we were all up here at the cabin—his family, my family. Just another holiday in my mind. You couldn't believe my surprise when I found my sister making out with Danny in this bathroom. Apparently they fell for each other when they were co-stars in *The Neverlanders*."

"It was a terrible movie." The corners of his mouth turn up in a smirk, and a warm wave courses through my being.

"It was a fantastic film," I disagree, but I secretly like the fact that he said it was bad just to protect my feelings.

"You're right. I own a copy. But if you want, I'll burn it. I will burn the living crap out of it." His fingers brush under my eyes, and I realize I'm crying. The tears are streaming down my face. Clearing my throat, I go back to patting Kayden's neck, studying his reddened skin instead of his sad eyes staring at me. I chuckle and shake my head back and forth. "It would have been our fourth year anniversary when Lisa announced she was pregnant with Olivia."

"That's messed up."

"You know what's even worse?" I whisper. "When we were kids, I told her I wanted to name my first kid Olivia after Olivia Newton John because I love the movie *Grease* more than life. And I just sat there for a moment wondering why Mom was crying happy tears. Why Dad was pouring everyone drinks and cheering. And why wasn't I enough?"

Kayden takes my hand and we both stand up. He hovers over me and backs me up against the wall. The palm of his hand grips my chin and his face edges closer, so close I can feel his breath hitting my lips with every exhale he releases.

"Before we walk out of this bathroom and I become Richard again, can I say something to you as Kayden?" he asks. His eyes are intense, zoned in on me, and I have a strong feeling that if he were to look away I would crumble into nothingness.

"Yes," I mutter, almost breathless by his touch.

"You're more woman than Danny could ever have handled." His thumb brushes against my lips, parting them. "You're more of a sister than Lisa deserves. Your parents are talented as hell in movies, but they're blind to the truth of real life." My heart picks up speed as time somehow stops completely. He inches closer and kisses my falling tears away. "And I am one lucky bastard to be your made-up boyfriend."

I don't know what to say, so I smile like a goof ball, feeling my stomach fill with all kinds of wonder. When words come to mind, I let them fly from my mouth. "You give the best pushed-up-against-a-wall pep talks."

"Hey, do you see that?" he whispers, and I cannot help but take in every syllable he speaks, every word he somehow sings.

"See what?"

He looks up and points right above us. "The invisible mistletoe hanging above us."

My cheeks heat up and my eyes move to the invisible mistletoe of his imagination. I love his imagination. "Well, look at that."

"You know legend says it's bad luck if two people stand under the invisible mistletoe and don't kiss."

"How much bad luck are we talking?" I smirk, feeling his hand tighten around my back.

"Well, I can't say exactly. It's different with each person. But the last time, a guy I work with who didn't kiss under the invisible mistletoe grew an extra finger and lost a toe. No lie."

The serious look on his face makes me want to crack up laughing, but the way his fingers are massaging my back makes me want to do everything in my power to avoid the bad luck. "Well, we wouldn't want that, now would we?"

"I guess not…" He takes one finger and runs it up and down the side of my neck, making me sigh softly, wanting the invisible mistletoe to travel with us everywhere we go.

When his lips slowly discover mine and my fingers run through his hair, my mind starts begging for more than his soft kisses. He presses his hips against mine, pinning me to the wall, and his hands become entangled in my locks as he deepens thc kiss. I feel all of him against me, almost forgetting where he begins and I end. His tongue slowly slides into my mouth and I sigh with ecstasy, feeling his warm hands wrapping around the edge of my shirt, slowly pulling it up. When he pulls it all the way off of my body, he stares me in the eyes and moves my hair behind my ears.

"I hate how they make you doubt how amazing you are," he breathes against my lips. I watch as he gets down on his knees and moves my arms to the sides of my body. Swiftly I try to move them back to cover my stomach, but his green eyes demand that I lose this battle. "Eyes closed."

His words are commanding; but, it sounds more like a request than an order. And, I abide.

My other senses become fully aware of all of my surroundings while my eyes are closed. I can hear my family chattering from the dining room, and I pick up on the sound of the wind from outside hitting against the house. My lips part and I can taste the air being sucked into my lungs. I smell the shampoo in his hair—coconut. And I *feel* him. His hands are placed on my bare sides and his forehead is resting against my stomach.

I relax all of the muscles in my body the moment I experience his lips kissing around my belly button. My mind shuts down, and I get rid of all of the other senses that are no longer of importance. I commit to Kayden's touch. His fingers effortlessly massage my sides. His tongue caresses my skin for a split second before taking refuge back in his mouth. His soft lips deliver countless shivers. My hips choose to motion toward his lips, but he doesn't take advantage of their brainless actions. His hands stay on my hips as he rises to his feet, and I can tell he's hovering over me again. I just don't know if I currently have the strength to witness him before me yet.

"You're perfect," he says before slipping me a gentle kiss. His voice is confident that he's telling me a fact, not simply his opinion. "Okay?"

I open my eyes to see him reach for my shirt, which he places back on my body. He turns away and he doesn't look back at me. He just opens the bathroom door and disappears.

He thinks I'm perfect.

I smile, because he wasn't Richard—he was Kayden.

And it wasn't an act.

Walking out of the bathroom after collecting my thoughts, I plan to head back to the dining room to try to make this night end quickly. Before I can even round the corner, I'm standing right before Danny. Not saying anything, I try to edge around him, but he blocks my exit. "Is there something I can help you with?"

His brown eyes look at me the way he used to look at me—as if he cares. It pisses me off because I never know what's going on in his head, when he's playing a role, when he's being himself. Truth is I never really knew who Danny was.

"Is it always going to be like this?" he asks, leaning against the hallway wall, the heel of his shoe resting against the wall trim. "Is this awkward air always going to be between us?"

"You know what's disgusting?" I wonder out loud, crossing my arms across my body. "These past few years I've been waiting for an apology. For you and Lisa to say, 'Sorry, Jules. The way we behaved was out of line and disrespectful.' That's all. But every time I come around here everyone acts as if I'm the crazy one. And I hate you so much, yet there's still this weird amount of love floating around in my gut. Which in turn makes me hate myself a little more."

Danny reaches to touch my face, but my raised eyebrow and hands on my hips make him rethink his move. "We were happy. You made me happy, Jules."

"No, I totally get it. I wasn't successful enough to stay attached to you. Which is fine. Whatever. You're shallow. I get that. But…my *sister*?" The tears that are burning in the backs of my eyes are winning the fight tonight. Lisa turns the corner holding Olivia in her arms and I sigh. "My sister?"

Lisa and Danny give me this look that embarrasses me. They look so sad for me. They pity me. And the waterworks flow. Lisa's lips part to speak, but nothing comes out. That's the closest she's ever gotten to looking a tiny bit remorseful for her betrayal, but the look disappears when she shifts to Danny.

"I'm putting Olivia to bed. Join us when you're done going down memory lane." She hisses her final words and I roll my eyes.

"He's done." I turn to Danny who still has that look of despair attached to him. "*We're* done."

Lisa rolls her eyes and walks away. Before I can turn to do the same, Danny's hand lands on my wrist and he hands me a phone. "Richard's phone was going off in his jacket, so I grabbed it to give it back to him. Then, I noticed he had all these missed calls from people called 'Chick with Blonde Hair', 'Brunette Girl Who's Crazy', 'Good Sex' and names like that."

I know it's all made up, my relationship with Kayden, but the idea of those girls calling Kayden hurts me more than it should, and it makes me think that everything has been an act. The pep talks, the invisible mistletoe. How could I think it was more? I just met the guy and I'm paying him a thousand dollars to date me for five days.

"He doesn't seem like the type of guy you need. I just—I don't want you to get hurt, Jules."

"Well, Danny, you should have thought about that before banging my sister."

I move to the bedroom Kayden and I are sharing and see him unbuttoning his shirt. He must have heard my footsteps because he begins talking without turning toward me. "Dinner shut down early, which is probably for the best. Everyone could probably use some rest."

I slowly close the door behind me, and when I see his shirt leave his body, I gasp. He's hot with a shirt on, but without one, he transforms into a superhero. He turns to see me gawking, but I don't stop. There's this tattoo lying on his chest of a coin—a penny.

When I finally tear my eyes away, I feel conflicted on just about everything. For a second I'm thinking about Kayden, but then thoughts of Danny flood my brain. My mind is confused, shuffled up because of all of these feelings of past regrets—and disgust in myself for still caring about those regrets.

His lips turn down and I move closer to him, resting my hands on his chest. My head is quick to fall to his chest, too, when he wraps his arms around me.

"I'm going to ask you something," I whisper, and I'm positive he can feel the tears falling against his chest.

"Anything," he says, stroking my hair. "Anything you need. Let me know."

"Make love to me?" I ask, looking up into his eyes. "I know it wouldn't be real, but I'm fine with that. I'm fine with fake love making." I'm begging for him to touch me gently, to caress me in his arms, and to kiss me as if I'm the only person in this world he would ever want to kiss.

His body cringes against mine before he pulls back. He turns away from me and runs his hands through his hair. "I can't do that."

"Yes you can. I'll even double your pay if you want." I pull my shirt off of my body and toss it to the side of the room, walking closer to him. "Don't worry. It won't be real. I promise it will be meaningless." My hands attach to his sides and he brushes them off faster than they land.

"Don't, Julie," he hisses, using my real name. "I don't want to do this."

I'm mortified by his rejection. Pulling his cell phone out of my back pocket, I hand it over to him. "Good Sex called twice. You might want to call her back." I walk over to my suitcase, unzip it, and look for my pajamas. Christ! Of course the only ones I packed have puppy dogs, penguins, or Santa on them. No surprise Kayden doesn't want to touch me.

"Really? You're upset because of some names in my cell phone?" he asks, moving over to me. I keep digging through my suitcase, even though I've already found what I need. "You're upset that I have a lot of sex? I'm sorry. I didn't know that was part of my job description—letting you know all about my sex life."

"No, that's not it. I just don't see why you can be so screwable for them, but then I ask you for the same thing and it's a big no."

"It's been a long day. You're sleepy." I see him sit on the edge of the bed. The way his muscles become even more noticeable when he's pushes his hands into the side of the bed makes me blush.

"I'm not sleepy. I want some meaningless sex from a guy who seems to be a pro at that task." When those words leave my mouth, I want to slap myself because I sound like such a raging bitch. His hands dig deeper into the bed before he pushes off of it. He moves over to me and grabs my arm, pulling me into his direction.

"What do you want, Jules? You want meaningless?" His voice is harsh, rough around the edges, and I flinch at his intensity. "How do you want it? *Hard*? *Aggressive*?

*Fast*? *Deep*? You want me to pull your hair, unzip your pants, and slide off your panties without saying your name once? You want to wake up the next morning alone? Feeling hopeless yet again?" His hands wrap around my waist and he tugs my hips toward him. His voice softens and his touch becomes gentler. "Or do you want me to make fake love to every inch of your body? Telling you how I am the luckiest man alive to call you mine? Do you want me to take my time with you? Whispering sweet-everythings into your ear? You want my lips to kiss yours in such a way that makes it hard to tell where yours begin or mine end? Then do you want to fall asleep in my arms and wake up around two a.m. and make fake love with me all over again?"

He steps away from me, leaving my brain foggy, and he slides his hands into his jeans pockets.

"Or do you want me to be Danny? Because I pride myself in being a pretty damn good actor, let me know what role I'll be playing. The meaningless man-whore, the hopeful and endless lover, or the pathetic ex-boyfriend who used you and left you to become this weak thing before me."

I'm insulted by his words. He could've said no and left it at that, but no—he had to make me feel like a fool. "Fuck you," I whisper.

"*Exactly*, sweetheart!" he sings, clapping his hands together. "You just tell me how."

"Ugh, do you have to be such an asshole?"

"Do you want me to be? Because, clearly, I'm an actor. I'm unattached to feelings, to real emotions." He gestures toward the closed door, "I'm just like them."

My feet fidget against the floor. "I didn't say that."

"You didn't have to."

I feel terrible, because I *am* terrible. I've managed to disrespect and piss off the one and only ally I have in this place. What's wrong with me? "I'm—I'm sleepy," I mutter, filled with my own self-hatred.

He sighs, picks up a pair of sweatpants from his suitcase, and nods. "Me too." He heads for the bathroom attached to our room and when the door slams, I stomp my feet against the ground.

Idiot!

Changing into my puppy pajamas, I hop into the left side of the bed, covering myself up with blankets, including my head. I hope by the time Kayden re-enters he'll think I'm sleeping.

I hear the turning of the knob and peek out to see him staring at me.

"I know you're not asleep in the two minutes I've been gone. But I do apologize for the way I spoke to you." I don't say a word, and he moves to the right side of the bed before pausing. It's a big bed, so there's enough distance between us to make it a little less awkward—but it's awkward nonetheless. Picking up a few blankets and pillows, he moves over to the large couch that is lying against the wall. Good—sharing a bed would be a little too real for me.

"I'm sorry, too. For being—"

"—Crazy? Twisted? A lunatic?" He lists all of my very blatant characteristics, and I can hear the smile in his voice. I smell the mint scent of his toothpaste and wish I weren't such a dummy, because I really could use another Kayden kiss.

"I was going to say for being sleepy, but crazy works." I laugh, and I hear him snicker, too. Pulling the cover from over my head, I turn to find his face resting in my direction. There's a large gap between our bodies, but I feel as if we are already holding one another. "Did we just have our first fake fight?"

He nods. "For a first fake fight, that was pretty short-lived. We really have to work on that. Maybe more screaming next time."

"Maybe a little more name-calling, shoe-throwing, to edge it up a bit. Make it more believable."

A grin makes its way to his face, and he turns it back toward the ceiling. A period of silence follows, but it's not weird. It seems natural actually, the ease of not talking, a comfortable silence. I never had that with Danny. I always felt as though I had to entertain him, to stay interesting in order to keep his attention. Truth of the matter is, there was nothing I could have done differently—he wouldn't have loved me the way I wanted him to. You can't make someone fall in love with you just because you fell in love with them first. Before Danny I never realized how dangerous this emotion is—how lonely love can truly be.

Kayden clears his throat and moves around on the couch cushions, trying to get comfortable. "My older brother's last girlfriend came on to me once after a bad fight they had. I was still trying to find a new place, and I was crashing on his couch for a few weeks. I mean, Landon was a shitty boyfriend to her, spent more time working than next to her. She deserved better. They both did."

I listen, not judging his story, believing he wouldn't share such a memory with me for no apparent reason. I watch his partially closed lips as he continues telling his story. "After the last fight, Landon stormed out, calling her 'bitch this,' 'bitch that,' some nasty things. And I was sitting on the couch, confused as hell on what I was supposed to do. Here was this broken girl with tears streaming down her face. So I moved over to her and held her, feeling her weak body fall against mine.

"After calming down her wrecked self, I led her to the couch and we talked. About anything but Landon. I tried my best to make her smile, to make her laugh, because I'm almost certain there's nothing more beautiful than the sound of a woman's laughter. Then I told her she deserved more for herself and that no one should ever speak to a woman the way Landon spoke to her. I don't know if I sent her the wrong signals or if she was just so messed up in her head, but she crawled over to me, tried to kiss me. Said I was the brother she always wanted."

"What did you do?"

"I sent her home. I mean, yeah, my brother's an asshole, and sometimes it's hard for me to stomach the idea that we're related, but there's no way in hell I would mess around with his girl. There are supposed to be rules about this stuff. Ya know? Lines you never cross."

"I guess my family never got the memo on those rules."

"Mine either. I told Landon, when he got home—how Jasmine had tried to come on to me—and he called me a liar and kicked me out. Said he had a call from Jasmine saying that I hit on her and tried to have sex with her. He believed her over his own brother because 'that's what Kayden does.' He screws chicks and leaves. I didn't even try to explain the situation to him; his mind was made-up. It was right then that I realized he wasn't my brother. He never was."

"Why do you say that?"

"Because"—he inhales deeply and exhales slowly—"genetics make you related, but loyalty makes you family. Turns out the only family I have are my mom and my aunt."

I laugh. "And your made-up girlfriend, jerk." He smiles and runs his fingers through his perfect hair, pleased by my comment. I feel terrible for the way I spoke to him earlier, ashamed really. "I didn't want meaningless sex with you."

His lips curve up. "I know, and I didn't want you to want to have sex with Danny."

I nod once. "I know."

"Maybe after all of this is over, after I'm not Richard, and you're more…emotionally stable. Maybe then I can ask you out." He speaks with such certainty, such truth.

I laugh again. "It may take me a while to become emotionally stable."

He looks at me, his green eyes soft and still a bit puffy from his allergies, and when he turns away to face the ceiling, I follow his gaze, staring up at the ceiling fan that remains still.

"So what happens next?"

"Oh, I don't know. I mean, if you're willing to wait for me, then I can figure out my life. And you can take me to a really nice restaurant maybe. And do you dance? I love to dance. My last boyfriend made me think I loved video games but I despise them. I actually have no clue how to use the damn things and—"

"Jules?" Twisting my neck in his direction, I wait for him to continue his thought. "I meant what happens next with this family trip."

"Oh…" Just when I think I cannot embarrass myself any further, I one-up myself. No need to buy blush anymore. These red cheeks come with the territory. "Well, tomorrow for the girls there's cookie making and hot cocoa—I bring Bailey's to slip into mine. And for the guys, you go cut down the best trees—yes *trees,* as in more than one—and then each couple decorates one. The best tree wins a trophy, because clearly, what's a Stone' family get-together without awards?"

"Sounds nice."

"It was." I remember all of the fun years I had with Danny, doing all of those Christmas activities together. Then I think about how different it will be this year, watching him perform those tasks with my sister. But I have Kayden this year; I'll do my best to make believe with him. "It will be nice."

"Jules?" Kayden's voice comes out as a question, just as it did before I embarrassed myself with my overactive imagination of a world with him in it.

"Yes?"

"I love to dance, too. The older music, the better the music. Boys II Men, Hall and Oates, Temptations."

My hands fly over my heart, because I'm sure it's about to zoom out of my chest. "Stop, stop! You had me at Hall and Oates. When Lisa and I were kids, we stayed at this cabin with my grandma whenever Mom and Dad were filming. Grandma would always take us girls to old record stores, and of course I bought Hall and Oates's second album. I would play it over and over again. It's perfection. So…okay. Favorite song at the count of three. Don't think about it, just say. Ready?"

"Ready."

"One…two…three…"

"*She's Gone*!" we both holler, and I toss my hands up with excitement after hearing his reply. "Kayden Reece, I hate to say it, but…I think we just became best friends."

"This is the fastest moving, all-over-the-place relationship I've ever had. First we are madly in love, and now we are best-friends status. All within ten hours."

"There's only one life to live. Might as well live it up!"

A silence fills the room and the darkness of the room overtakes me, bringing on a new wave of sleepy thoughts. I close my eyes, thinking that Kayden is on his way to dream, too. Until, of course, I hear him humming the tune of *She's Gone* to himself. Then the lyrics follow. His voice is smooth and rich—in every note is a new found lust I have for this 'co-star' of mine. I can't help but join in at the chorus of the song, singing the high parts as he takes on the low in perfect pitch.

My cheeks are so sore from smiling so big for so long, and I catch a mad case of the giggles as his voice goes deeper and deeper. I never knew I could love Hall and Oates so much more.

When the sounds of our voices fade out and the stillness of the air summons us to complete silence, I relax against the mattress. I hug my pillow and curve my body away from Kayden after watching his eyes shut. Before I close my eyes, I realize a new personal truth.

Someday I'll be fine. Maybe not right here and now, but someday I will be able to look at Danny and not think about all the what-ifs. Someday I won't feel like the outcast in a world full of lovers. Someday I'll wake up in a bed, by myself, and be perfectly content with my life.

Yup. Someday I'll be fine.

When I wake up, it's still pitch-black outside. Turning on my cell, I see that it reads three thirty-four a.m. The snow is falling gently now, the sparkling flakes hitting the edges of the window as if stylishly choreographed in an intricate dance. I look over to the sleeping beauty, watching her body rise and fall. She's a handful when she's awake, but she's flawless and perfect in her sleep.

Rising from the uncomfortable sofa, I cringe as my scrunched-up body tries to unknot itself. Before assuming a full-upright position, I rub the back of my neck and roll my shoulders a few times to loosen up. I'll definitely be taking the floor during the next few nights. The couch isn't cutting it.

Slipping into a pair of shoes, I grab my coat and a pack of cigarettes and head to the front porch. The cold air momentarily takes my breath away, and for a brief moment, I consider going back inside where it's nice and warm. Zipping my jacket and pulling up the collar against the frigid air, I cannot help but wonder what I'm doing here, in the middle of nowhere Wisconsin, in the company of Oscar-winning actors. Why did I agree to this in the first place? First of all, I wanted to tell my parents that an agent had signed me, as if that would somehow prove my worth to them as an actor—and as a son. But when I heard the desperate pleading in Jules's voice as she stood on the chair in the lobby, begging for an actor, I recognized that desperation as my own when Stacey turned me down at the agency.

I rub my lips together before lighting up the cigarette and inhaling the first hit. That first drag normally brings an intense feeling of relaxation as the smoke fills my lungs; and, exhaling empties me of all tension. Usually, there's a pleasant buzz—a momentary dizzy feeling—that accompanies each drag, but not this time. I look at the cigarette, and wonder why I hold on to this nasty habit. Why I even started. But whenever the smell of smoke envelops me, whenever I breathe in the scent of smoke that remains embedded in my clothing, I remember her.

I was seventeen when I first fell in love. It was the last time I fell, too. She was two years older but just as dark, just as broken. We both grew up in homes where we didn't fit into the family portraits. We were the outcasts, the rejects, the creative types. Penny always believed in better days. She said that someday our acting careers would take off, and we'd show our families how much we didn't need them to believe in us.

She was more intense than I was, more…passionate. She was also more damaged, more lost. She wanted more than anything in the world to prove that she wasn't the negative space her family painted her to be. I wish she had been a little stronger, had a little more fight. There came a point when I realized that all of her passion, all of her bravado, was an act. She did not believe in herself. She saw herself as invisible. How her family portrayed her had become a self-fulfilling prophecy.

I never thought I would be the one to land the agent, to actually give this acting thing a real run for its money, but look at me now, pretending to be someone's boyfriend.

Penny would've laughed at this whole situation. Her laugh was contagious, spreading into my bones, infecting my soul. I guess I haven't quit the cigarettes yet because they remind me of her, her kisses, her scent. Of her sadness.

I toss the cigarette into the snow, and hear it hiss as the snow melts around its glowing tip. I should let go of the whole smoking thing; yet, there's this melancholy feeling that when I do, it means I'll let go of Penny and lose all of my memories of her and of us.

And I'm not sure if I'm ready to walk away from it all just yet.

Arriving back in the bedroom, I gaze at the beautiful blonde sleeping in the bed and a part of me wants to forget Penny completely. A part of me wants to move on from my past and get to know Jules. She's weird, emotionally scarred, and semi-annoying—in the best possible way—but I love those things about her. *Love those things?* Is that even possible? To love characteristics of a person you don't even know? The gulf between the couch and the bed mocks me as I crawl into the bed, and wrap my legs and arms around her. What am I doing? And why wasn't the cigarette enough? Why is it that, on this cold winter night, Jules Stone is the only thing in my mind that can bring me the warmth I'm searching for?

Gently kissing her ear, I whisper against it. "Sunshine…"

She shifts in her sleep, but not before relaxing against me, snuggling her curves even deeper into mine. I wonder if she knows I'm this close, if it would scare her. Does it scare me a little? I want her to wake up, roll over, and notice me. I want her to be all right with the fact that I'm this close.

I kiss her ear again, and she wiggles against the bed sheets and turns toward me. Her sleepy blue eyes slowly open; then open wide, startled with alarm and fear. "Ah!" she screams in shock, sitting up in bed and kneeing me in the gut.

"Ow!" I whine, grabbing my stomach, bending over in a small bit of pain.

"Oh my gosh!" She shakes her head back and forth, hands over her mouth, trying to dispel her dream state and waken more fully. "Kayden, I'm so sorry! But what the hell are you doing?! Do you sleep-walk?"

To be honest, I have no clue what the hell I was doing, why I chose to climb into bed with her. Jesus! I probably came off as a fucking psychopath just now. I don't snuggle, I don't hold people, and I don't let people hold me. So why in the hell did I climb into that bed with Jules? And why in the hell did it feel so…right?

"I'm sorry, it's just…never mind…I can't even explain it."

With her body turned toward me, all I want to do is kiss her over and over again. She shifts her eyes to the window, noting the darkness, and a yawn escapes her beautiful lips as she lies back down. “Kayden, it’s still sleep time. Go to sleep, Sexdorable.” she breathes out as she closes her eyes, and her smile widens. There’s so much I want to do to her, with her, right at this moment, but I can’t, and it pisses me off.

“Are you awake?” I mutter, sitting cross-legged on the bed next to her almost motionless body. It takes everything for me to not burst out laughing when I see her eyes reopen with a sassy look of attitude.

“I’m not nice when I don’t get sleep.”

“I’m hungry.” Moving over to her, I take her arms and pull her up into a sitting position.

“I will punch you in your face. No lie, I will fuck you up,” she warns, trying to edge back down to her pillow. I can’t help but laugh at the grump, and pull her up again, holding her against me.

“Let’s go make something to eat. Seeing how I missed dinner because you almost killed me.”

“Really?” She leans her head on my shoulder, and I feel her hot breaths slapping against my neck. *My gosh…I really like holding you.* Her body wiggles even closer to mine, making me think she somewhat likes me holding her, too. "You're playing the 'I almost died' card? At like four in the morning?"

"It's three, and yes, I am."

Her hands rub across her face, and she slaps her cheeks back and forth, trying to wake herself up. "Fine. But you're cooking."

I yank open the fridge and see what I have to work with. "How do you like your eggs?" I ask, pulling out the carton.

"Sunny-side up. At eight in the morning." She mopes around the kitchen in her slippers and damn cute puppy dog pajamas, and I snicker at her tired attitude. Her hair is all frizzy and wild, and her make-up is smeared across her face, but I don't mention it. It's kind of cute, and it works perfectly with her early morning personality.

"Pancakes it is," I say, pulling out all of the ingredients. Jules hops on the barstool across from me, and watches as I start mixing everything together. "Chocolate chips or blueberries?"

"Blueberries." Her fingers open the blueberries and she pops a few into her mouth. Her nose wiggles at the tartness of the fruit and she shakes her head. "Chocolate chips."

As I start to prepare our early-early breakfast, she lays her head down on the kitchen island, watching all my moves. Even though she doesn't say a word, her body language speaks for her. She's comfortable and relaxed around me—as if we have always awakened at three in the morning for breakfast dates. Her lips hold a soft smile upon them, showing me that she's pleased I woke her from her dreams. For some odd reason, I feel as if I'm still dreaming.

"Why don't you have a girlfriend?"

Her question should be random, but I'm surprised she hasn't asked before. I turn on the skillet, dreading the idea of turning my body toward her and answering her. The words are there, my reasons are clear, but I don't want to talk about it. Our eyes finally meet and we stare for a moment, neither of us blinking, neither of us *wanting* to blink. Until I turn away and go back to making pancakes.

She doesn't push the subject, but I can tell she's still wondering. "You cook a lot?"

"I used to." My reply is curt, and I feel bad about it, but I can't go into more detail. Tossing a few pancakes onto a plate, I slide it over to her and pull out the syrup from the cabinet.

"Thank you," she yawns, covering her lips with her hand. "There are a lot of things about you that you don't talk about, aren't there?"

"There are a lot of things about me that I can't talk about. Otherwise, I'll turn into you and someone will need to pin me against a wall, feeding me a pep talk." Turning off the stove, I grab my plate of pancakes and join her at the island.

"I give pretty decent pep talks."

"I'm sure you do, I just don't *receive* pep talks very well."

"Oh my gosh." Her eyes close as she takes the first bite of the pancakes and I swear it looks like she just had a moment of personal pleasure. "Three a.m. pancakes shouldn't taste this good. *No* pancakes should taste this good." My insides twist in a knot knowing that she enjoys them, creating some kind of weird satisfaction within me.

"You smell like smoke again," she blurts out, eating her food.

"I'm trying to quit."

"Why did you start?" Another question left unanswered. She blinks once, and when her blue eyes look up, I ease myself away from her in the opposite direction. She notes the new distance between us. "I'm sorry, I get personal. I'm nosy. Sorry." Her apology is authentic, but it's not necessary. She has no reason to apologize for my personal issues. There's so much of my history I've learned to block out of my world, and there's no reason for me to revisit it out loud. Inside my head those demons are free to float around, but the idea of the words actually leaving my lips is terrifying. There's such a realness to talking about Penny, and about what happened, that it scares the living hell out of me.

"I wish I could be more like you. Able to shut up and forget things." She stares at her pancakes, cutting them into pieces. "But I gotta say I also wish I knew more about you, about your history. It's safe to say I fall for guys fast. I become weak searching for love or lust. Any emotion, really. But it's different with you, Kayden. With you it's hard to find the weakness inside of me. With you I feel strong. So, I simply wish I knew more about you, because you make me stronger."

"What do you want to know?" I ask.

"Anything. It doesn't have to be personal at all. I just want to know more."

I cut my blueberry pancakes as she forks her chocolate chips, and we both open our mouths, feeding each other a bite. She arches a mischievous smile and I laugh. Then we each lift our plates and switch our pancakes around.

"I believed in Santa Claus until I was ten." My confession doesn't seem too thrilling, but her smile is so wide that I'm almost certain I can feel my face heating up from her joy.

"Are you trying to tell me that Santa isn't real? You bite your tongue with those satanic lies!"

She's wide awake now and more sexdorable than ever. "I also didn't vote during the last election."

"Un-American and Un-Santa. I'm so happy you're only my made-up boyfriend. Because clearly this relationship would never work. Come on, what else?"

"I may or may not have thought it was ridiculously cute when you farted in your sleep."

Her hands rush to cover the horrified expression on her face. "Shut up!" She shoves me in the arm and I cannot stop laughing. "Shut up! Are you serious?" Nodding, I continue eating. She shoves me again, and her cheeks are now the color of a tomato. "Did it smell bad?"

"Kind of like old burritos."

She starts to giggle, and then she bursts out into laughter, her head flies back, and she snorts. Again. I've never been so happy to hear snorts. "That makes sense because I had tacos for lunch." It's weird, sitting here, talking about her farting. Most girls would be extremely embarrassed, and she was for a moment, until she turned around and started cracking up at herself. Her laughter makes me want to join in. Jules Stone is somewhat addicting.

I stare at her lips as she chews her last bites of pancake. I move closer to her, mere millimeters away from her face, and without thought, I run my tongue against the side of her mouth. Her body stills, and her doe eyes widen in a sudden shock. I pull back quickly. "Sorry, there was some syrup." Moving her finger to the plate, she wipes up some syrup, and smears it across my cheek. Then she does it again, only this time it runs down my neck. When her tongue strokes my cheek, it takes every ounce of my willpower not to lift her up and carry her back to the bedroom. Her tongue retreats back into her mouth momentarily before she bends forward to lick the syrup from my neck. Her sticky fingers brush against my lips, and I lick them clean, sucking gently on the tips.

"Let's go build a snowman." Her random comment is the complete opposite of what I want to do.

"No."

"Let's go build a snowman," she repeats, standing from her stool and pushing her body against mine.

I laugh. If I don't laugh, I'll kiss her and then she might realize that I want to kiss her as Kayden, not as an actor in a make-believe scene. "No."

With that, she turns those irresistible, pleading puppy-dog eyes on me, and her bottom lip drops to a pout. She places her hands on my chest and whimpers, "Please, made-up boyfriend who I am made-up in love with? Pleeeeze?!"

How can I say no? How can I turn down the pouty lip and the puppy-dog eyes? She knows I will give in. She rushes back to the bedroom, glancing over her shoulder to make sure I follow, and gives me the matching hat, gloves, and scarf she packed for me.

Yup. Matching hats, gloves, and scarves for both of us. The hat has some weird fur on it, and when it goes on my head, I'm pretty sure I've just lost at least seven points on the manliness scale.

"You're so cute." She grins, looking at my ridiculous accessories.

" You don't call guys cute. You don't call them adorable and you don't call them cute," I argue as I step into my boots.

"Even if it's sexute?" She pauses, tapping her finger against her nose. "Okay, so sexy and cute don't work as well as sexy and adorable do, but still. You look like the type of guy I would love to roll in the snow with."

I narrow my eyes in on her and follow her into the living room. Pulling her fur hat onto her head, she smiles my way. "It's *faux* fur. When I was a kid, I saw this documentary about what they do to get the real fur, and let's just say I'm anti-fur. And anti-watermelon…but that was a different documentary." She's so fucking weird and I hope she never changes. I think the world could benefit from more people like her, more weirdness. Plus, she looks pretty damn sexute herself in her winter getup.

"Well the faux fur goes perfectly with our faux relationship." When I say this, I see the corners of her mouth turn down for a split second before she reverses her frown and reaches for my hand.

"Let's go."

How is it already colder than it was when I walked out earlier for a smoke? I even have more layers on, and I'm pretty sure my dick is a popsicle. Why couldn't we stay inside, licking syrup off each other? I like the licking of the syrup.

Jules is already knee-deep in the fluff, balling up snow as I stand on the edge of the drive-way watching her go at it. All the trees surrounding the cabin are decked out in white Christmas lights, and it's a perfect setting for a perfect scene. The way she smiles as she continues to build a snowman is the most beautiful thing I've ever seen in my life.

Sliding my hands into my pockets, I sway back and forth. "Her name was Penny," I blurt out. The world comes to a halt, everything freezes, and the sounds of my own words fight me, wanting to rip me apart, but I remain standing. The only thing keeping me upright is Jules staring back at me, interested in what I'm saying, interested in the words that are forming sentences, that are forming my history right before us. "My grandmother gave me her engagement ring before she passed away. It was six years ago, and I was planning to propose to my girlfriend Penny. I had it all planned out, some real romantic crap…flowers, music, tears. She was supposed to meet me at our favorite restaurant and she never showed. Penny had a lot of personal demons that she fought constantly. She tried to overcome them, but that night she lost the battle and overdosed."

I see Jules's eyes filling with tears, and the burning sensation in the back of my eyes is painful; but with effort, I don't break down.

"I don't talk about it." I laugh, but nothing's funny. I laugh because I'm still angry with her. I laugh because I'm still sad. I laugh because if I don't I will crumble. Every part of me will fucking crumble. I laugh exactly for those reasons, because nothing's funny at all. "I never talk about it."

Jules studies me, tilting her head to the left, trying to find something, trying to find me. "You blame yourself?"

"Every day, every night, every moment." I squeeze my eyes shut and shake my head back and forth. And when I reopen my eyes, Jules is much closer; she's marching closer to me, taking big strides through the snow. Her mittens are covered in snow, and her arms wrap around me. She holds me, and I allow it. All I want her to ever do is let me hold her in return.

"There's nothing you could've done differently. It's not our job to fix people. We *can't* fix people." She pulls me closer and my arms wrap around her, breathing in her fragrance. "It's simply our job to love them, even when they're broken. No matter what you could have done, no matter how much you told her you loved her and that she was enough, it wouldn't have made a difference. You couldn't save her. People have to save themselves."

I kiss the top of her faux fur cap and thank her, even though a thank you will never be enough.

She wiggles in my arms and pulls away a tiny bit. "Yeah well, there was a time I was talking to a stranger while driving to a cabin and he told me that no one was coming to save me and that I had to save myself. I get the feeling he was onto something." I barely notice the cold air that still surrounds us. Jules nudges me in the arm and holds her hand out to me. "Come on. Follow me."

She leads me into an untouched layer of white snow and stands shoulder to shoulder with me. "What are you doing? What are *we* doing?" I ask, and she smirks.

"The first Christmas after my grandfather passed away, Grandma and I lay out here and made angels for him. Now lie down on your back. We're making snow angels." Before I can reply, she plops down into the freezing flakes and spreads her arms and legs, moving them back and forth to create her snow angel. It seems so fitting too, because she is an angel. Somehow I stumbled across this astonishing earth angel, and I cannot tear my eyes away from her.

Her soft voice orders me to lie down, so I follow suit, losing myself in the moment. When we have both created these snow angels, we lie still and hold hands and gaze up to the dark, starlit sky.

"This is for her…for your angel who's stronger today than she was before. Merry Christmas, Penny."

As the tears flow freely from my eyes, I turn my head away from her so she won't see them. Our fingers tighten against one another, and effortlessly, she sends waves of warmth through me, and touches my soul.

I'm still angry at Penny for the choice she made, for not fighting harder, and then I become angry with myself because how do I know she didn't fight? I'm still sad, and wish I could have held her one last time and told her everything would be okay. Yet Jules makes it a little easier to forgive, to not fear the sad memories, and to not allow the angry feelings to overtake me.

The snow picks up and floats down on our faces, painting us with its beauty before it melts away. I part my lips to taste it, the wetness of the night gracing us in the moment. It's therapeutic, this moment. It's real, and it's very much needed after all of these years of never speaking about it. If anyone should be paying anyone, I'm pretty sure I owe Jules a check.

My heart beats a slower rhythm, and it's easier to breathe. It's beautiful, this made-up relationship.

Before we stand to move toward the house to dry off, I look up to the sky one last time to see a few stars shining in my direction. Perhaps the stars in the sky are loved ones letting us know they are nearby, guiding us through the night.

Merry Christmas, Penny.

# 6 Jules

## Grandma Got Ran Over by a Tim Faulter

Soaking wet, we make our way to the bedroom, leaving puddles of water trailing through the cabin. I can't stop thinking about what Kayden shared with me, of how he opened up to me. If we could make believe forever, I know I would never tire of the sound of his voice and the stories he tells. He's intriguing and intense, but he's equally just as humorous and sweet.

I would never have imagined that the tattoo on his chest had such meaning associated with it. When he opened up to me, I saw it, the cracks inside of him. The hurt. I feel honored and immensely grateful that he allowed me to enter his private world.

Grabbing a pair of black sweatpants and an oversized t-shirt, I head to the bathroom to change while he changes in the bedroom. Sliding out of the wet clothes, I toss them into the tub, a problem I will deal with at a later time. Staring into the mirror, I study my wild hair and the eyeliner that is awkwardly spread across my face. In the past I would have cared about guys seeing me look like a hot mess, but with Kayden I don't care at all.

It feels good to not care.

Then I realize I *do* care—a little at least. As I leave the bathroom, I kind of hope that Kayden wants me. Okay, that's a lie. I *need* Kayden to want me, because I want him so bad. I miss his taste. I crave his touch. I can't help it—he's everything I've always wanted and nothing I've ever had. Pulling my hair together, I toss it into a high ponytail, and I wipe all of the make-up off my face. Holding my hand in front of my face, I do a breath check, blowing into my palm. Holy crap! I have monkey ass breath. I am heavily suffering from morning breath with a mix of pancake breath, and a dose of *what-the-freaking-hell-is-that* breath. Gross face. Reaching into my duffle bag, I pull out my zipped up toothbrush and paste and prepare to kill mega things that decided to live—or die—within my mouth.

After disinfecting myself from head to toe, I open the door and see Kayden standing there in a white Henley shirt and a pair of grey sweatpants. The way the shirt hangs from his body and the sweats fall against his hips makes my lady parts want to follow him until he allows me to taste every single part of him.

"Can I tell you something without it being weird?" he asks, rubbing his hand against his jawline. What a perfect jawline it is.

"No. Please make it weird. I like weird. I *love* weird." He crosses his arms and smirks, and I am almost certain that my heart has never loved the idea of making someone grin more in all its life. If I could, I would make it a daily routine to make those lips curve up in pleasure.

"I lust you, Jules. I lust you *so hard* right now. It's almost impossible for me to be around you and remember that this is all an act. I just, I haven't felt…" His shoulders shrug up and he bites the bottom corner of his lip. "I haven't felt anything in such a long time. I avoid my feelings like the plague. I sleep with random girls to forget about emotions, to get lost in the act of sex, to make those kinds of moments lose their true meaning. I haven't made love in years, but after meeting you, I want you to know that I may consider it someday in the future. I may consider falling in love again, because I like the way I feel when I'm with you.

"I want you to know I appreciate the fact that I can talk to you about who I am and where I come from and not feel awkward about it. I appreciate that I can kiss you and not want to retreat after the kiss. I really appreciate how whenever I make you laugh I feel like a better man. I know this isn't real or anything, and I know I may be suffering from actor's syndrome where you fall in lust with your co-star. But dammit, if I had to be in a fake relationship with someone, I'm really fucking happy it's with you."

When he finishes speaking, I sit quietly and contemplate what he has just shared with me. The way each word replays in my mind makes me glow from the tip of my head to the bottom of my feet. "I lust you, too." We stare at each other, and momentarily, I forget.

I forget about all of the past hurts. I forget about all of my insecurities when it comes to guys. I forget that right here, right now is all an act; and I allow myself to fall so deeply in lust with this stranger I feel I have known all my life. It feels so damn good to be forgetful.

"Hot cocoa?" he asks. I bite the bottom of my lip, and glance toward my cell phone, seeing that it's almost five-thirty in the morning.

"Hot cocoa."

Entering the kitchen to see our pancake mess still there is pretty nice. *It wasn't a dream.* This is simply the weird, awkward, totally ridiculous life I'm currently living. Moving to the cabinet, I reach up to grab the mugs and feel two hands land on my waist.

"I don't want hot cocoa," Kayden whispers, his lips ever-so-slightly touching the edge of my ear. Twirling me around, I meet his stare. He brushes his finger against my chin and my insides churn in frenzy. His green eyes focus on me, and I cannot tear my gaze away from him even if I want to. He's smirking with such a strong sense of knowing that I wouldn't want to be anywhere else on this planet.

"Kayden…" I whine with pleasure as he brings his lips close to mine, millimeters apart, and our breaths comingle into one. His hands wrap around my waist, and he lifts me onto the top of the marble counter. Any minute now, Dad will be around to start his six a.m. coffee pot. Mom will wander down the steps of the isolated cabin soon after, wanting her peppermint tea, her chocolate croissants. "We can't…" I whisper, pulling him closer to me, rejecting the very definition of my own words.

He doesn't kiss me, but I want him to. I want him to kiss me in a way that makes real lovers cry out of mere jealousy. I want him to hold me the way he's never held anyone before. My back arches my body toward him, pressing me against his chest, making our bodies become one.

I don't know how we got here; I don't even fully understand *why* he's here in Wisconsin with me. Why did I even decide to hire an actor? Why did Stacey decide to sign Kayden that day? Call it a moment of weakness, call it a dark period in my life—or hell, call it fate. All I know is that within the past twenty-four hours Kayden Reece has interjected himself into my life and I am oh so glad he did.

He wraps his hand around my neck, pulling me closer as he separates my legs, stepping in between them. His lips brush across mine, and my eyes want to close, but he warns against it.

"Stay with me, Jules. I want to experience all of you. I want to smell your strawberry lip gloss. I want feel your smooth thighs. I want to get lost in those blue eyes, I want to hear all of your whispers, listen to your secrets, and I want to taste your lips against mine." When he kisses me, he makes sure I'll never forget it. I run my hands through his hair, light moans fighting to escape my covered mouth. His hands run up and down my back, holding me still against the countertop.

He kisses me as if we have been doing it all of our lives. He kisses me as if he wishes to do it until the day we die. He kisses me as if he's so deeply in love with me and he fears that it will be the last kiss we will ever share.

And I kiss him back. Ohhh do I kiss him back… Wanting nothing more than his taste, his body, his words. I kiss him back, wishing to know how his mind works, why his heart beats. I kiss him back, knowing that, even if we say this thing between us is only an act, it's far from the truth.

The steps from upstairs start to creak, giving us our first warning signals. He allows for our lips to find comfort against each other one last time before he pulls back and gives me a smile that melts me faster than the rising sun melts the fallen snow. He turns me into a complete pile of mush, and I'm absolutely, positivity crazy about the feeling of being his mush.

*Creak. Creakkkk.*

His eyes move to the mess we made with the pancakes and the batter from earlier. "You want me to clean this up?"

I shake my head as he helps me off the countertop. I smooth out my outfit and nudge him in the opposite direction of the footsteps, toward our bedroom. It's fine if I'm caught in the kitchen, but being caught with my fake boyfriend would just be awkward for me.

One last kiss to my nose and he disappears.

Nothing about this moment is counterfeit. Nothing about our intense connection can be tagged as a lie. Kayden may be my made-up Christmas boyfriend, but he's far from being just an act.

That's when I hear "Stop it, Tim!" followed by a fit of giggles and the sound of people crashing into the hallway wall. "Get over here, sexy. Mama wants to taste you some more."

My hands shield my wide-open mouth. Oh my gosh! That's Grandma's voice saying some really disgusting, disturbing things. I pause and then shift my body back and forth, trying my best to think what to do next, attempting to figure out how to not throw up at the thought of my grandmother tasting someone.

Oh my gosh. *Gross*!

Their stumbles get closer and I slide to the ground, hiding behind the kitchen island.

"That's right, baby. Slap Mama's booty. *Harder*!"

Involuntary gagging starts now. You ever have a fantastic dream and then it slowly creeps into a nightmare? And there's no way whatsoever to wake the hell up? Story of my night.

Kayden re-enters the kitchen through the same door by which he had just exited, and sees me crouching on the floor. "Jules, what are you—"

"Shhh! Get down here!" I whisper in panic. If I have to listen to Grandma getting some, Kayden should be by my side suffering with me! He slides down to join me just in time to hear a deep male voice call my eighty-year-old grandmother his naughty Tinkerbell, and I swear to God I pee my pants a little. It's like in those horror movies when the killer is right around the corner from you and you are so afraid that you tinkle just a little out of fear.

The footsteps are closer and I know they are inches away from us. I can feel the island shake when this mysterious Tim character pushes my grandma up against it.

"It looks like someone made us breakfast. Here, try this pancake," Tim laughs.

"Ohh, get the syrup. Pour it on right here," Grandma moans. Oh my gosh I swear Grandma just moaned and everything about making out, lust, and sex is officially ruined for me. And I never want to see another freaking pancake in my life.

"Who is that?!" Kayden whispers, and my head falls to the palms of my hands.

"Some random guy, and my grandma."

When I look up at Kayden, his face is contorted in laughter, which he is trying his best to control. My fingers find his skin and pinch him hard as I send the look of death to him.

"Tim, why don't you get some ice cubes?" Grandma coos. My eyes shift to the refrigerator sitting directly in front of Kayden and me. Kayden's face mirrors my 'oh shit' face, and we edge closer to one another, curling into a tight ball, trying to make ourselves smaller. Maybe he won't see us?

*Creak. Creakkk.*

This Tim guy is getting a lot closer, and I instantly hate him because he ruined the specialness of my early morning pancake date by feeling up my grandmother with pancake syrup. It isn't until Tim's back is to us that the knot in my stomach forms and I realize that this Tim guy is much, much younger than Grandma. He's also shirtless, and I see syrup dripping down his neck.

Ewwww!

When he pulls out the ice tray and his body swivels around, it's almost impossible for him to miss us. He looks down, our eyes lock, and I gasp along with Kayden. It's not just some random Tim guy—it's Tim. As in Tim Faulter from the television show *Goners*.

He doesn't say anything, but a smirk is plastered on his face. He tips his invisible hat at us, and all I do is wish that I am invisible, too.

He moves away from us, toward his eighty-year-old girlfriend, and I hear her squeal at what I assume is the ice cubes finding her body.

Cue the return of the involuntary gagging.

"Okay, okay, okay! That's enough!" Standing, I wave my hands around and around to stop whatever the freaky-freak is happening on the other side of the island. Grandma's eyes find mine and she smiles so sweetly.

"Oh hey, baby!" she sings, as if she's not aware that she just scarred me for life. "What are you doing up?"

"What?! Are you kidding me?! What are you doing here with *Tim Faulter*?!"

Tim has that same goofy grin that Grandma has on her face, as he extends his sticky hand toward me. "Oh, so you know my work? Nice to meet you. Joyce has been telling me some great things about you."

Did he just call her Joyce?! Grandma doesn't *have* a first name! And I'm definitely not touching his sticky fingers. The idea of where those fingers have been is quite disturbing to say the least.

"I thought you were going to be in the Alps for the holiday?"

"Why in the hell would I be in the Alps? I'm always at the cabin for the holiday. Your mommy dearest was throwing a big hissy fit about me bringing Tim along, saying it was supposed to be a family gathering, but I figured, what the hell? It's my damn cabin, I'm a grown woman, and I can bring whomever I want into this place. Besides, she said you were bringing that Richard guy along, and no offense, but he's not exactly family."

Tim leans over the island and looks down to Kayden. "I'm assuming you're Richard."

Kayden slowly rises and looks as if he's been caught by his parents doing very bad things. "Yeah."

Grandma's eyes send this weird wave of energy to Kayden, and she places her hands on her hips. "Who are you?"

He distributes his top-of-the-line smile her way and his long eyelashes blink once before those sexy eyes reappear. "I'm Richard."

"No you're not."

I feel every hair on my body stand up straight at Grandma's simple comment. "Yes he is."

Her sassy attitude almost sends me away to my room in despair. "Julie Anne Stone, do you really want to stand in front of me right now and lie straight to my face?" My gaze falls to the ground and I feel her stern look staring me down. "Don't make me ask again," she warns.

"His name is Kayden," I mutter, watching Tim eat our leftover pancakes.

"And how do we know Mr. Kayden?" Grandma uses her scolding voice and now I feel like I've been caught in a terrible act.

"He's an actor from my agency."

A short laugh is heard first, followed by a landslide of laughter that gives my grandma the hiccups. "You hired an actor to be your boyfriend?!" More hysterical laughter is heard as she bends over in a fit, as though I am the funniest clown in the room. Seriously though, it's not that funny. "Oh my…Just when I think this family cannot become anymore dysfunctional."

"How did you know it wasn't Richard?" I ask.

"You texted me some weird picture of some nerd guy wearing a headset that said 'I love my Richard.'"

Ohh, so Stacey really didn't get my picture of Richard the other night. I owe her an apology.

Grandma walks over to me and kisses the top of my head, leaving me confused and afraid until she says, "I'll keep your little white lie a secret, Granddaughter." Her eyes travel to Kayden and there's a soft grin on her face. "If you hurt her, I will cut off your penis."

With that, she takes Tim's hand and walks off, leaving me to witness the terrified expression her final comment has left on Kayden's face.

Heck, if I were him, I'd be scared shitless, too. I'm kind of surprised Danny is still alive after what he did. Kayden doesn't blink, and I chuckle at his fear. "We should get to bed for a few hours. Today's going to be a long…long day."

Before we can leave, Tim rushes back into the room, grabs the bottle of syrup, smirks, and tips his invisible hat again before disappearing.

Mother-flipping gross.

"Sunshine, wake up." Kayden's lying next to me, and I can feel his body heat radiating against mine. When my eyes open, his greens smile and I can't help but want to kiss him. "Good morning."

"Good morning, indeed." I wiggle out of the comforter and sit up on the mattress.

"Ah, you're a much happier morning person now." His hair is dripping wet and he smells like coconut shampoo. Dang, if I would have woken up a few minutes earlier, I could have 'accidently' walked in on him in the shower.

Well, there's always tomorrow for the accidental walk-in.

"You see that window? And the sunlight shining on the snow? That's why I'm happier. Because it's actually morning, loser."

"Oh…" He edges me closer to him and wraps me up in his arms like I'm his to protect. "You're much more of a loser than I am."

"Kiss my ass, jerkface."

"Fuck off, freaky-ass freak." He hisses as I lean against his chest. I love the way he smells...I love the way he feels. Mostly though, I love how he tells me to fuck off and calls me a freaky-ass freak.

"Bite me, asshole," I bellow, playfully slapping his cheek with the palm of my hand.

He lays me down on the bed, and his body hovers over mine. His hands are pinning me down, and I never want to get up. "I would, but you would like it too much."

*I would.* "I wouldn't!"

"Is that a challenge?"

I nod once and stretch my neck out. His fingers run up and down my neckline before his teeth lightly begin to nibble on my neck. *Oh, fuck my life…That feels good.* I feel new levels of excitement, his gentle caressing fingertips give me goose bumps; and Kayden knows he was right that I would like it. He's slow at first, sucking gently in one spot before his teeth run across my skin. A moan escapes my parted lips the moment his tongue leaves his mouth and explores my collarbone. His kisses get deeper, and a growl emanates from his throat letting me know that he loves biting me as much as I love being bitten. His hands fall to the hem of my t-shirt, and when his fingers make contact with my stomach, my back arches toward him, silently begging for more of his soft caresses, more of his bites.

OhMyGod. I'm lusting so hard right now.

I get it now… It all makes sense to me, why Bella was all gaga for Edward and shit in *Twilight*, because he made her *feel*—the same way Kayden is making me *feel*. If he looked at her the way Kayden looks at me; if he touched her the way Kayden touches me; if he nibbled into her soul the way Kayden did mine, then I would expect nothing less than to be transformed into something that would be his forever.

Kayden's eyes find mine, asking permission to remove the shirt, and I have it off and tossed to the side before he can even blink once. Next, I reach for the sides of his shirt and remove it before he can blink twice. The penny on his chest stares right at me, and my finger circles it, slowing down time. I feel his heart pounding, and my hand lies over it. Breathing deeply and slowly, he closes his eyes and gently places his hand over my heart. Matching breath for breath, my hand rises and falls against him as our hearts beat as one.

He sits up and moves to the other side of the bed, away from me. When I push myself up on my elbows, I turn to him to find such sadness, such regret, lying inside his eyes.

"I can't sleep with you, Jules." He bends his knees, resting his elbows against them, his eyes staring at the comforter wrinkled underneath him. His breathing is heavy, and I only wish I could read the thoughts flying through his mind. He rubs the bridge of his nose before he looks at me, and my heart shatters. He looks so hurt, and I worry I'm the one who's hurting him.

"Did I do something wrong?" I push myself up and sit cross-legged, positioning myself directly in front of him. He brushes a piece of fallen hair from my face and through tight lips, he slowly releases the breath he's been holding.

"No. That's the thing. You've done everything right. All of these former assholes you dated used you, treated you like shit, and put their hands on you for their own greedy needs. And I hate them for that. For making you doubt yourself. I hate that they touched you like they meant it. I hate how they looked at you as if you were the only thing they saw. And I hate how much you gave of yourself to people so unworthy."

I don't know what to say to him, but I've never felt so exposed in my life. My arms wrap around my body, and Kayden lifts the comforter, quick to cover me up.

"You deserve more, and I don't deserve to touch you. At least not the way I *want* to touch you—not yet, anyway." He holds his hands toward me, palms up, and stares into my eyes. I place my hands against his, and unknowingly he changes my life in an instant while he keeps talking.

"You deserve to have your hands held. You deserve to be taken out to a nice restaurant. You deserve to go dancing because you fucking love dancing. Then the lucky bastard who gets to do all of these things with you should walk you home and stop at the front steps. He should want to make love to you, but he doesn't even really let the thought cross his mind. He kisses you gently, with no tongue, and no longer than a five-second peck. He pulls away from you, smiling because he knows the simplistic kiss was the best thing that has ever happened to him. Finally, he walks back to his car, telling you he'll call you, which he does. He calls you the moment he hits his car, just to thank you for allowing him to know you."

"Why do you always say the right thing?"

"I don't. But after meeting you, I realized how much meaningless sex I've had with girls who were probably as hopeful as you are. So from the head master of the Meaningless Club to the head mistress of the Hopeful Club, I apologize on behalf of all the losers, users, dumbasses, dicks, fuckers, meatheads, nerds, liars, cheaters, and just plain idiots."

Best apology ever. "Well, we Hopefuls fully accept your apology."

"Good," he sighs, and I see him really taking in my acceptance. His body relaxes, and he edges closer to me, "Now get dressed. It's already two in the afternoon. I gotta go pick out some Christmas trees with your ex-asshole, Tim Faulter, and your dad, and *you* have to go bake cookies. Then later on, I'm going to be the best boyfriend ever and make everyone in your family super jealous of our fake relationship. You have no idea the kind of things I have planned for these next few days."

He hops off of the bed and rubs his hands together, emitting some Dr. Evil laugh as he heads out of the room. When he suddenly comes back, he pauses and reaches into his back pocket, pulling out two folded pieces of paper.

"Oh, also, I ran into your cute little niece—who by the way was fully clothed today—and we had a nice talk about how she thinks you're her favorite aunt."

"I'm her only aunt."

"Geez, do you always pay that much attention to *all* the details? Anyway, we each drew a picture of you." In his left hand, he holds up the first piece of paper, which is a very colorful drawing of swirlies and weird marks that make no sense whatsoever. In his right hand, I see a drawing of pink stick figures.

"Let me guess. You made the swirls?"

His mouth hangs open and he gasps. "How the hell did you know?! Anyway, back to planning the best relationship day ever. Mwhahaha!" He marches off again with his evil laughter.

He's so odd.

I hope he never changes.

"You're just in time. Grandma and Mom are in a heated fight over the fact that she brought Tim Faulter to the cabin." Lisa smiles my way, and I honestly can't think of the last time we actually spoke without some snarky remarks, but I'm still on my high from Mr. Kayden, so I'll be civil.

"Mom's overreacting."

"Mom always overreacts. She wouldn't be our mother if she didn't." Lisa sits on the stool at the island and I have a flashback of Kayden pushing me up against it. My cheeks heat up, yet Lisa doesn't notice as she starts flipping through the recipe book. "Remember when we took her car out for a drive and crashed into the neighbor's mailbox when she was filming in Florida?"

I chuckle. Of course I remember it. Mom still brings it up, about how embarrassed she was that we didn't tell her, and that she had to find out by seeing it on gossip magazine covers. It turns out that the paparazzi weren't too far away and caught our drive on camera, tagging Lisa and me as the troubled sisters. "I think we're still grounded from that."

"Yeah, but luckily we only have ten more years left with her disappointed eyes."

"Until we crash her next car."

Lisa laughs and I can't help but giggle with her as we relish the memory. I haven't laughed with my sister in such a long time…

Moving to the fridge, I open the door and pull out eggs and butter to get started with the baking.

"How have you been, Jules? You and Richard seem really happy." Lisa stands on her tiptoes to reach the mixing bowls in the cabinet and my gut whines at her comments.

The refrigerator hangs open and I rest my hand on the top of the door. "Lisa, I don't think I'm really at the point where I can do small talk with you."

"Right." She shifts her body around and smiles a sad grin my way. "I'm sorry. I just…Do you think we'll ever get to that point?"

`"I don't know. But…" I bend down, look into the fridge, and pull out a big jug, placing it on the counter. Grabbing two glasses, I turn to Lisa and give her a halfway grin. "Dad made his spiked apple cider. And I am at the point where I can get drunk with you if you want while we bake an absurd amount of cookies that no one ever really eats."

I pour two large glasses of Dad's Christmas 'punch,' which has been known to make you forget the rest of the day, and slide one over to Lisa. In the past, I would have said something snotty to her when she approached me asking how I was. Probably something like, 'I was fine until you stole my boyfriend' or 'Doing great. How's sex with my ex?' But this time, I wanted to do something different. I remember that Kayden told me to do the opposite of what I used to do in order to be able to move on.

I want to move on from this, and if that starts with getting drunk with Lisa, then it starts with getting drunk with Lisa.

Holding my glass up, I tap it against Lisa's. "To drunk dysfunctional families."

"Hear, hear."

Mom comes hurrying into the kitchen in a frenzy, her hair all messy. "*Mom, drop it*! I'm not going to keep talking about this!" She sighs, and Grandma enters right behind her.

"Tina, you answer me when I'm talking to you! Why on earth is it such an issue to have Tim here?!"

"He's not a good person. That's all I'm saying. Look, Mom, I get it. You're lonely ever since Dad passed away. But you can't keep going around hooking up with these creeps just because you miss Daddy."

Grandma laughs a deep-throated chuckle, grabs the glass out of my hand and downs it, slamming it back against the island. "Your father, rest his soul, and I hadn't had sex since you were four years old. I haven't been touched in almost fifty-five years! So if I want to run around like a whore, I will run around like a whore and not be judged by my snob of a daughter who clearly hasn't gotten any in a very long time. I feel bad for Matt. His poor hand has to be tired by now!"

"Whatever, Mother. As if you have gotten any. Kissing on a man half your age doesn't count."

"For your information, I got some in the bedroom last night, in front of the fireplace, in the dining room, and right here on top of this island. *Twice*."

My elbows, which are resting on top of said island, slowly retreat as my early morning gag fest begins to return. By this point, I'm pretty sure Mom is about to flip the hell out.

"You're disgusting. I can't even talk to you when you're like this. Do you always have to be so…" Mom huffs and puffs and tosses her arms around, kicking invisible stones, looking like a crazed woman. "Ugh!" Wow, Grandma makes her feel exactly how Mom makes *me* feel. It must be genetic.

"Tim told me about how you hit on him way back when you and Matt were on a break. How he wasn't interested. Does it hurt your feelings that he chose me? Honey, you two never even knew each other."

*Mom hit on Tim, who's now dating Grandma? Mom and Dad were on a break?!*

"I hit on him? Is that what he told you? Why Tim Faulter, anyway? Did you ever stop to think why a Hollywood sex god would be interested in an old fart like *you*?" Wow, I wonder if Mom knows how bitchy she sounded in that moment. Grandma's face drops into a hurt expression for a moment. When the look dissipates, so does Grandma, leaving the room.

Mom rakes her fingers through her hair, doesn't even look toward Lisa and me, as if she hadn't even noticed we were there in the first place, and she storms off toward Grandma. "Mom! I didn't mean it like that!"

Lisa and my eyes meet, and the blank expressions on our faces explain exactly how we feel about this awkward situation. "More apple cider?" I offer, and she holds up her glass as I pour us both a refill, this time to the rim.

# 7 Kayden

## All I Want for Christmas

"You sure you can handle that axe?" Danny chides, watching me stand in front of the tree I chose for Jules and me to decorate later that night. Ever since we arrived to the tree lot, I've felt Danny's eyes following me like a weird-ass creep.

"I got it," I smirk while trying my best not to roll my eyes at the idiot who let Jules get away. Oscar winner or not, he's still an idiot. When I raise the axe to begin hacking at the tree trunk, I sigh in annoyance when he comments on my technique.

"You're going to put out your back."

"I'm not."

"The way you're swinging that thing around, I bet you fifty bucks you put your back out."

He's baiting me, and I can tell he's intimated. "It's killing you, Danny. Isn't it?" I start hacking away at the tree, strike after strike pretending that it's Danny's head. "Seeing Jules happy? Seeing that she didn't need you to be happy? You probably thought she was some weak girl who would walk around for the rest of her life, crying for you to love her. It must piss you off—"

Whack. Whack. Whack.

"—so much that she doesn't need you or want you anymore. She's free of your bullshit." I look up to him staring at me. "Free of your fucked up bullshit."

He laughs. "You think you know Julie after dating her for what, six months or some crap like that? I had her for three years. Last night she told me she still loved me, you prick. So if you think that Julie is anywhere close to falling for your bullshit lies, think again. She's not over me, and she never will be. I mean, she's dumb, but not that dumb."

The axe drops and I'm standing in front of the short dick in less than a second. "Don't ever talk about her like that."

He keeps laughing, taking some pride in my revved-up annoyance. "Mr. Accountant, take it easy. You and I both know Jules isn't the sharpest tool in the shed."

My hands ball into fists, and my heart rate skyrockets. My blood is boiling and my body is shaking because I know if he doesn't take it back I will be forced to knock the asshole out.

"What?" he says, stepping back from me. "You going to kick my ass?"

Damn straight I'm going to kick his ass.

"Richard, please. You don't want to fight me. If you do, you might end up in a hospital bed."

"Put me in a hospital bed. *Please, do it.* Because if I'm in a hospital bed, then that means your ass is in a body bag."

Then it gets weird. Like, really fucking weird. Danny jumps back, and poses in some kind of odd cat stance. "Listen, fucker. I've taken tai chi for over five years. I almost have a black belt in karate, and I am known to be a lethal weapon to small villages."

I pause, relaxing my fingers. "Did you just use a quote from *The Neverlanders*?"

He drops his weird pose and rests his hands on his waist. "No shit. You saw that film?"

"Of course I saw it, asshole. All of America saw it."

"Actually it was an internationally acclaimed movie. Many more people outside of America saw it and—" He's quick to shut up the second my fist makes contact with his face. The blood starts trickling from his nose and his hands shoot to his face. "*What the fuck, Richard*?! You actually hit me?! Are you a fucking wild man?! Jesus! Have you ever heard of talking things out?!" He's whimpering like a little bitch, and I get a small dose of pleasure from it.

"Don't ever say anything negative about Jules again. Got it?" Picking up my axe, I go back to chopping down my tree.

"Fine. Jeez. What kind of an accountant are you anyway? I'm an actor! This face is my income!" he shouts, wiping the blood away from his nose.

When the tree falls, Matt walks up to us and smiles. "That's a nice tree you got, Richard. Looks like Danny's tree might have a little competition."

I turn to Matt and grin. Out of everyone so far, he's the most normal. "Thanks. I think Jules will love it," I say back to him. Danny narrows his eyes at me, and looking like a sad kid who just lost a fight, he walks off toward the truck.

Matt moves over to the end of the tree and begins to lift it up as I lift the other side. "I don't know if you know this, but Jules is a fantastic actress. One of the best out there, and she was about to have her breakthrough moment a few years ago, I know it. After what happened with Lisa and Danny, she walked away from it all, claiming that Hollywood was responsible for the two of them betraying her. I can't exactly say what made Danny and Lisa do what they did. And I could never imagine what Jules is going through, but when *you* look at her, it's as if she forgets those two. She forgets everyone." He pauses, setting the tree back down in the snow. I drop my side too and listen to him continue speaking.

"I wish she would remember how much she loved the craft and give it another chance."

"Have you ever tried talking to Jules about the Lisa and Danny situation?"

A short smile appears on his face followed by a shrug. "How do I even approach the issue without it seeming like I'm taking sides? I love both of my daughters more than life itself, and a part of me dies every time Jules refuses to come home because they can't stand being in the same room together."

I nod in understanding; it has to be tricky ground to walk on. "No offense, Matt, but did you ever think that by not saying anything it appears you have chosen a side? And that side isn't in Jules's favor."

Crestfallen, his face reveals his understanding of this sudden realization. "She thinks I chose Lisa over her?" His hands fly to the back of his head, and he marches around in the snow, cursing under his breath. When he turns to face me, his blue eyes are brimming over with tears. "How do I fix it? I wouldn't even know what to say, where to begin."

I bend down and lift the tree trunk back up. "Don't worry, Matt. I'll help you figure something out. You're an actor, a damn good one, too. So we'll do what you do best. We'll rehearse until we get it right."

Matt bends down, picking up the other side of the tree and lifts it up. "Thank you for finding Jules. Thank you for seeing what I somehow missed."

"I'm wasted," Jules says, spinning around and stumbling toward me when I walk into the kitchen after pulling all four Christmas trees into the cabin with the guys. She's giggling like a school girl with her sister Lisa, and I swear I somehow entered the *Twilight Zone*.

"You are, aren't you?" I say to Ms. Drunk Girl.

She wiggles her nose and nods. "And we made cookies!" There are at least three trays of burnt cookies, and she bites into one of them. "They're burnt because I can't cook, not because I'm drunk."

"It's true. She's a terrible cook."

"Says the girl who slept with my ex-boyfriend!" Jules screams, and the room fills with an awkward silence until the girls start cracking up in a laughing fit.

"How much did you two drink exactly?" I ask, rubbing Jules's shoulders. I don't really need to ask, because I can spell the rum on her breath.

"Enough to make it possible to stay in the same room together," Lisa says, eating the burnt cookies. "Enough to kind of feel like sisters."

"Well," I sigh, "keep drinking."

Jules's laughs fade away when Danny walks into the room and kisses Lisa. Her eyes change from the playful drunk to the saddened one, and I pull her arm toward me.

"You're fine." I whisper and she snuggles against me, still looking at them.

"I'm fine," She turns toward me and gives me a smile, "I'm going to go shower, try to sober up a bit. I'll see you later to decorate the tree?"

"Yeah, of course."

I hate this, I hate that she's hurting and there's no way to make it better. There has to be something, anything I can do to make it better.

I was wrong when I said Matt was the most normal of the Stone family—he's not. He's just as screwed up as the rest.

"Mr. Stone," I say, clearing my throat as I sit in his office, and he paces back and forth in the closed off room.

"Matt. Call me Matt." He keeps pacing, rubbing his chin, and my eyes fall to the ground. This family is really making it easier to respect my own.

"Right, Matt. Uh, we don't have to look at this as a real rehearsal or anything." My eyes move as fast as they can to meet his. "You don't have to rehearse this naked." The fact that I've seen Matt naked before I've seen Jules's body is all kinds of fucked up. I have no words for the level of discomfort soaring through my veins.

His hands land on his hips as he stands in front of his desk, and all I want to do is vomit for the next fifty years. "I do my best brainstorming naked. I *need* my best brainstorming for this. Besides, people were born naked. Why is it that society acts like it isn't normal? Anyway, let's get started." He pulls his desk chair around toward me and crosses his legs.

I was wrong again. I want to vomit for the next one hundred years.

"I've been playing the words over and over in my head, and I think I figured it out. So in this scene, I want you to be Jules, all right?" His eyes are locked with mine, which is fine because I have no desire to look anywhere else.

"Okay."

He rubs his hands across his thighs and then reaches to hold my hands. Fuck my life. "Julie Anne Stone. You're my everything and I realize I haven't been there for you the way I should've. I've let you down when you needed me the most. There's this weird thing that happens in life where people become so terrified of the outcome that they choose to not speak up on the matter. They don't stand up for those who have been silenced. I should have stood up for you.

"I should have held you close, and even though I couldn't have made things better for you, I should have let you know you were not alone. I can't say I understand what your younger sister did, and I will never try to justify it. I can't say I support her choices, but I can say I love you both equally, fully, and unconditionally." Matt's hand lands on my cheek, and I can't help but be so spellbound by his speech, by his words, that I completely forget he's naked. I forget that I'm Kayden. I forget everything but the words he's speaking. He's not only saying the words. He's feeling them. Matt Stone is a fan-fucking-tastic actor.

Next, he moves my hands over his heart and continues his speech. "You're my heart, and I just need you to start beating again."

Fuck it, I'm crying. Yup, I'm crying, and I'm not ashamed to admit it. Those were some beautiful words right there.

"What the hell is going on?!" The door swings open, and Matt and I turn toward it to find Jules standing there with the most extreme expression of 'what the fuck' plastered on her face. Quickly I yank my hands away from Matt's chest and stand up.

"Oh my God. Jules, it's not—"

Matt stands up and gestures toward Jules, who turns away. "Jesus, Dad! Put on your pants!" she screeches, covering her eyes. Moving over to her, I go to touch her and she jumps. She gives me a stern look and points her finger at me. "I get it. Dad rehearses naked. It's a weird norm around here. But what I need you to do right now…what I *really* need you to do is to go wash your hands before you touch me."

I chuckle because her cheeks are so high and so beautiful. “Okay, but you stay here. I think your dad needs to talk to you.”

As we sit on the living room floor in front of the roaring fire, Olivia shows me her favorite Barbie dolls and all of the accessories. When I say all, I mean all; there are at least fifty pieces of plastic clothing on the floor. Tossing some more pink clothes on the pinked-out doll, I start playing with her, walking her across the floor. “I’m Barbie, and I’m sooo pretty!”

Olivia giggles and tries to grab the doll, but I keep pulling it away from her, making her break out into a fit of giggles. She’s ridiculously adorable, and she reminds me of how much I miss Hailey and should make more time to hang out with my crazy little cousin.

“Give me that!” she shouts, placing her hands on her hips with extreme attitude, and I catch a glimpse of her mother in her. She arches an eyebrow, and I can’t help but laugh at her sassiness.

“I’m a Barbie and I’m awesome! I can’t wait to give Ken a big kiss!” Picking up the Ken doll, I make the dolls embrace and Olivia falls to the ground in an overreacting matter, grabbing her stomach and falling victim to an invisible tickle monster. “Muah! Muah!”

She snatches a Barbie from me and smiles. “This is alien Barbie. She looks like me!” She holds the doll up to her face and smiles.

My heart stops beating and all I want to do is wrap this little girl in my arms and tell her she’s wrong. “You’re not an alien, Olivia. But you are beautiful, just like the Barbie.”

She shakes her head back and forth. “Daddy says I look like an alien. I’m gonna be famous, he said.”

“Well, between you and me, your daddy is a fart-face-people-hating weirdo.” I start attacking her with tickles and she loses it into another giggling fit. “Besides, Ken loves you!” I scream, kissing her with the Ken doll.

“Oh my gosh. I was afraid this would happen. My family is driving you loony.” Jules laughs, walking over to Olivia and me. She lifts up her niece and becomes the tickle monster in the flesh. “Is he playing with your Barbies?! I thought only you and I played with these Barbies, kiddo?” She squeezes Olivia and covers her in kisses. When she stills her niece, their blue eyes meet. “You want to know a secret?”

"Secrets, secrets!" Olivia screams, jumping up and down. Watching Jules interact with the young girl makes me lust after her that much more. It's nothing less than adorable.

"There is a *BIG* plate of chocolate chip cookies on the counter in the kitchen and *NO ONE* is in there right now." Jules takes her finger and taps Olivia's nose. "And I bet no one would even know if one or two were missing."

Olivia dashes off, leaving Jules and me sitting in front of the fireplace. Jules relaxes onto the floor, smiling toward the running toddler. "There are a lot of things I regret with Danny and Lisa, but that little girl? She kind of makes it worthwhile."

"How did your talk go with your dad?" I ask, hoping that it's at least a start to better communication. Her cheeks turn red and she grabs the Barbie from my hand, leaving me with Ken.

"It was good.  Dad actually passed my name on to someone in LA about auditioning for a movie next month."

"Is that good?"

The way her smile grows and her dimples deepen, I know it's good. "I should never have given up. I shouldn't have given Danny and Lisa the power to stop me from chasing my dreams. Dad said you had a big part to play in this, too," she says leaning in toward mc, making the dolls kiss one another, "Thank you." Her eyes shift to the ceiling and a beautiful sigh leaves her lips. "Oh no. That damn invisible mistletoe is back."

I look up, shaking my head at the nothingness above our heads—which somehow stands for everything. I reach for her arms and pull her into my lap, leaving her no other choice than to wrap her legs around me.

"Merry Christmas, Kayden," Jules whispers before pulling her lips to mine and kissing me gently. Her lips are softer than I remember, and I cherish the short time they spend against mine.

"I don't want your money," I say as she pulls an inch away from me. I can still taste her on my lips, and I can't imagine losing that feeling after these few days. "I don't want this to be fake anymore. After we leave here and go back to Chicago, I want to take you out. I want to get to know you, and I want to slowly fall for you, taking in every detail of our adventures together. What I don't want is for you to fall for me right away. I want you to make me work for it, work for you because you need to be chased after, longed for, desired. I really want to date you, Jules Stone, so fucking badly."

Her eyes move to the ground and she looks sad—sadder than I've ever seen her look. Something's happening in her mind, and it's hurting her. "I want to date you, Kayden. I'm just not ready yet."

I nod, completely understanding. "Right, too soon." I bite the corner of my mouth and narrow my eyes. "What about now?"

She laughs a true Jules laugh and I feel my heart grow in size. After we leave here, I'm going to take time to figure out who I am, what I want to be.

And then I'm going to take this girl dancing.

A few hours have passed, and we move on to the tree decorating festivities, and I can tell Jules is trying her best not to appear hurt about the Danny and Lisa situation, but I see right through her.

"I'm not jealous." She peeks her head into the other room where Lisa, Danny, and Olivia are standing by their Christmas tree. Danny and Lisa are standing next to each other, looking at messages on a phone, and Olivia is getting tangled-up in tinsel. "I just sometimes think it could have been me. We could have been the happily ever after."

"You're overthinking things. Shake it off." I kiss her forehead and go back to lacing the lights around the tree.

"But don't you ever think about how things would be? If you and Penny were still…" Her words fade off and she squeezes her eyes shut. "It's nothing like that. I'm stupid. I'm sorry."

I don't reply, because I do think about it all the time—what life would have been like if Penny were still here. But all I can think is it would've still been hard, a struggle, a lifetime of trying to fit together when we were never meant to be in the same puzzle.

When I see Jules standing on her tiptoes, reaching to hang up a decoration, I sigh, thinking of how it could be with us. I also think about all the moments that Jules hasn't been the most important person in the room, how she has always been overlooked, and I want to give her that moment, to shine.

"Hey, can I give you your fake Christmas gift now?" I ask Jules, and I see her eyes twinkle with curiosity. Clearing my throat, I call everyone from the other rooms and Jules looks at me confused. I ignore her confusion, and everyone wanders into the living room and takes a seat.

"I just want to say thank you for inviting me into your lives, into your home. I've felt nothing but welcome, and I appreciate it. As you all know, Jules is stunning. She's beautiful inside and out. She's gentle, she's silly, and if she allows me…" I turn to Jules, taking her hand in mine and getting down on one knee. "If you allow me, Jules, I would be honored if you permitted me to love you for the next one hundred years. You make me unafraid of my past and so certain of my future." Reaching into my pocket, I pull out my grandmother's engagement ring. "Will you marry me?"

Tears fall from her eyes, and she covers her mouth with her hands. I know this is supposed to be an act, but it feels frighteningly real. In a good way, too. Her confused eyes lock with mine and she mouths, 'Really?' and I nod.

"Of course! Oh my gosh, yes!" she screams, and I leap off the ground, wrapping my arms around her. She kisses me, and I lose myself against her. Everything feels perfect. Everything is right. Up until we pull away and hear a cold silence in the room.

Turning toward everyone, I look to see their eyes staring at a cell phone—Jules cell phone.

"Jules," her mother whispers, looking up to us. "Richard just called twice. And he left you a message apologizing for breaking up with you the way he did. He also said he would pick up his game systems after the New Year."

The sudden shift of energy is ugly, and it happens so fast that I now feel like I'm falling. I'm falling into a pit of lies, and Jules is right there beside me.

# 8 Jules

## I Really Can't Stay

"You *WHAT*?!" Dad hollers, and I feel all eyes giving me looks of disappointment, their judgmental gazes on me. Everyone's shouting, everyone has an opinion, and I feel like disappearing through the front window. "Jules, are you crazy?! He could have been a murderer! You clearly lost your mind!"

"You don't understand!" I cry, but he's right. I wasn't thinking. I wasn't making any sense. I can hardly see Dad through my tears, and all I see is Mom tossing her hands around in annoyance.

"I can't believe you would do something so stupid! How could you be so freaking stupid!"

"Hey, come on. She was just trying to—" Kayden steps forward, but I block him.

"Look, Kayden, it's over, okay? The show's over. No need to cover for me. The fake relationship is officially done. You'll have your money by Monday morning." When I turn to him, his eyes look hurt, as if my words were meant to destroy him. They weren't. They were only meant to tell the truth.

"Yup, the act is over," he says, running his hands through his hair. His cell phone goes off and he reaches into his pocket and answers it, walking into the other room.

"I don't see why it's such a big issue." Tim Faulter is still here, and even he has an opinion on my craziness. "She was doing it to try to fit in."

"Oh shut up, Tim! As if you have any right to have an opinion on this family," Mom says in such a gross, mean way.

"Look, I'm just saying that I get it. Here Lisa is, sexing it up with her ex. I, too, would get drunk and find a fake boyfriend."

"Hear, Hear!" Grandma shouts, drinking from her spiked eggnog.

"Mom, shut it. You're drunk," my mom says to Grandma, rolling her eyes.

"And you're boring, but you don't see me pointing that out," Grandma snaps back at her.

Everyone's on different teams—either Team Fake Boyfriend or Team Jules is a Liar. All but Lisa. She's sitting silent, staring at me. Her mouth opens, but nothing comes out, and it shuts just as fast. When it opens again, a tear falls down her face and she whispers, "I'm sorry."

Her apology rips through my heart and sends me stumbling backwards. I turn to leave the room and all the shouting, when I see Kayden in the kitchen, running his hands over his face. He's shaking, holding the edge of the countertop to keep from falling. When I walk over to him, I know it's not because of the commotion in the living room, but because of something else. Something worse.

"What is it?" I ask, and when his green eyes look into mine, flooded with sadness, he clears his throat, trying his best to get the words out.

"My…my mom. She's in the hospital." He's falling short of breath, trying to collect his thoughts and not fall apart right there. "I gotta go, I gotta drive, I gotta…"

He's pacing back and forth and I place my hand on his shoulder. "Let's go."

I grab his hand and we move through the living room where everyone is still yelling their heads off, fighting, screaming, and noticing everything but us. Packing up our luggage, we load up the car.

"Let me drive," I say, and he shakes his head.

"You stay here. Don't worry about me." He clears his throat and digs through his coat pocket, pulling out a pack of cigarettes. "I'm fine."

"No you're not."

Opening the pack, he curses, throwing the empty box. "Dammit!" He marches around, kicking invisible stones and yelling in frustration.

"Kayden…" He's falling apart. He's about to shatter, and he's living alone in his mind, thinking about the worst possible outcome. Then he turns to me. Our eyes meet and his body stills.

"She's my mom…" he whispers. The reverence in his voice touches my soul. "She's my mom."

I wrap my arms around him, and hold on tight, feeling if I let go that he would vanish. "Let me drive, please."

We have been driving for three hours, and haven't really said a word to one another. It's all pretty sad. The fact that he had to be so far away when his mom landed in the hospital is my entire fault. I should never have tried to hire a made-up boyfriend.

"Thanks again for driving," he says, tapping his fingers against the passenger window, breaking our silence.

"Of course."

"I'm really sorry, too. About how things went down with your family."

I shrug and wiggle against his leather car seat. "It was destined to happen anyway. But on a plus side, I think I hate Lisa."

"And that's a plus?" he chortles.

"Oh yeah. Before I *fucking* hated her. But now it's just hate."

"Well look at that. Progress!"

I smile at him, and he gives me that killer grin back. Holding my hand out toward him, I feel him take it and hold on tight. Every mile I drive, I can feel our fake relationship fading away.  Stacey calls me twice during the drive, but I figure I'll call her when I get home because I refuse to ruin my last few moments with Kayden. We don't talk anymore until we arrive in front of the hospital. He looks toward the emergency room, and I can see his fear of the unknown.

"I'll come in with you," I say, pulling into the parking lot. He nods his head once, and we step out of the car. His fingers find mine again, and we walk inside. There's a lot of commotion inside—people crying, people sitting and waiting to be seen. When Kayden spots his family, his hand drops mine and he rushes over to a girl and wraps his arms around her.

I have no clue who the person is, but he looks better, kissing the top of her head and allowing her to cry into him.

When they pull apart, I see the girl saying that his mom is all right. Next, another guy walks toward Kayden with puffy eyes; he hesitates before wrapping his arms around him. When they do embrace, they hold on tight.

I release the breath I've been holding, and I realize our short made-up world has come to an end. Whatever fairytale love story we have created over the past few days disappeared the moment I parked outside. He's with his family now, and I need to allow that. I'm not part of this world, this story.

Moving toward the door, I exit the hospital and wipe the falling tears from my eyes. The winter chill mocks me as it pushes me around with its winds. My cell phone starts ringing and when I answer it, Stacey screams. "Where the hell have you been?! I've been trying to reach you for days!"

"Sorry, Stacey. Service up north sucks, Is everything okay?"

"Um, no…it's not. You took an actor from the agency?"

"Yeah, so? I told you that. What's the big deal?"

"What was his name, Jules?"

A knot ties up in my stomach, twisting my insides because the tone in Stacey's voice isn't promising. I turn toward the entrance of the hospital to see Kayden walking my way. "Kayden Reece."

I hear Stacey's heavy sigh through the cell phone as she plops herself down onto a piece of furniture. "Julie, Kayden Reece isn't with the agency. I turned him down due to lack of experience… He must have stayed in the lobby and…"

Stacey keeps talking but my phone falls into my pocket.

"Sunshine," I hear; and Kayden stands in front of me, concern showing in his eyes.

"Is your mom all right?" I ask.

"She was hanging up Christmas decorations and fell. She was unconscious for a while, but she woke up about thirty minutes ago."

"That's good. That's great, Kayden. One quick question though…" I sigh and find his eyes, locking into them, trying to see into who he really is. "Did Stacey sign you at Walter and Jacks agency?" I watch as his face drops and he realizes I know about his lie.

"I can explain," he insists, edging closer to me, but the closer he gets, the more uncomfortable I become. The deeper green his eyes become, the more confused my mind grows.

Was it always an act? What was real? How far would someone travel with a lie for one thousand dollars?

"It's okay." I smile, shrugging my shoulders. "It was just a business deal anyway, right? See, this is why I don't date actors. You never know if you're just a part of their show."

"Jules…" Kayden whispers in such a low tone that it's almost silent.

"You should go back inside to be with your family." My voice cracks, losing all its strength. I know it's time to let go, it's time to get back to what's real—to reality. "Merry Christmas, Kayden."

I turn and rush away as I reach in my pocket to pull out my cell phone. I'm quick to dial Stacey's number to see if she can come pick me up. I don't turn around to see if Kayden is chasing after me, because I'm positive he's not. He knows as well as I do that the act is up.

Waking up two days later without Kayden sleeping in the same room is kind of depressing. What's even more depressing is waking up alone on Christmas morning. I know it sounds crazy, but I even kind of miss my family's yelling. And the chaos.

But mainly I miss my car, which is sitting at a random gas station in the middle of nowhere Wisconsin. My life is way more dramatic than it was when I played video games with my boyfriend who is probably engaged to some Hanna chick by now.

Pulling myself out of bed, I stumble into my kitchen and glance at the counter where burnt cookies are lying. My eyes shift to the floor, and I notice wet spots leading into the living room. My heart tightens, and right before I let out a blood-curdling scream, I see Dad setting up a Christmas tree in the living room.

"What are you doing here?!" I yell as Mom jumps out of her skin on the couch.

"Julie Anne! You scared me!"

"You're scared? *You* broke into *my* apartment."

"No," she says, shaking her head, "your grandma did." Grandma, Lisa, and Olivia enter the room from the dining area, and I can't help but smile. "Listen, Jules. I know we're terrible people. We are all over the place, we make bad decisions, and we yell too much, but we are your family. And your family is going to sit here and spend Christmas with you."

My eyes fall on the Christmas tree. "It's beautiful." I say, moving to the couch with Mom.

"It should be. It's the one your fake boyfriend cut down. Where is—" Dad starts, but realizes he doesn't know my fake boyfriend's name.

"Kayden."

"Oh, that's much better than Richard. Where is Kayden?"

I glance at the engagement ring on my finger. I haven't taken it off, and it's a pretty embarrassing fact. I don't know why I keep wearing it, but the idea of taking it off saddens me. "He's with his family. Where's Tim? And Danny?"

"Tim is probably in the Alps right now," Grandma laughs, eating the nasty cookies. "He was an ugly motherfucker, wasn't he? And he had a small—"

"*Mom*!" my mother hisses as her cheeks redden from embarrassment at what my grandma almost blurted out. I can't help but smile at the dysfunctional lives that make up my family. Looking toward Lisa, I arch an eyebrow, wondering where her other half is.

Lisa lifts her daughter and stands near the tree as Olivia hangs some ornaments. "I figured we could use some true Stone family time, without Danny. He's in LA with his family for a few days."

"Lisa?" I ask, staring my sister in the eyes. She's younger than I, but the tiredness in her eyes shows. I wonder how long she has beaten herself up for falling in love with someone who was off limits. "I hate you."

Her eyebrows perk up and she smiles softly. "You don't *fucking* hate me, but you hate me?" I nod. She smiles wider. "Best. Christmas. Ever."

"Oh, and I got you a new car for Christmas," Dad says nonchalantly, tossing me a set of keys. "Kayden told me how yours broke down when we were 'rehearsing' together."

"I can't take—"

"Oh shut up already. Just take the damn car," Grandma hisses, opening a bottle of wine.

Well, I guess I'm taking the damn car.

There are things I've learned about families as a whole. They make mistakes. They say the wrong thing. They fall apart. But the ones who really care? They always try to pick up those pieces and glue them back together. Yeah, there are still cracks and it still hurts, but there are also laughs and love floating around. My family's broken but in the most amazing way.

I plan to be dysfunctional right along with them forever.

New Year's Eve comes in, my family flies out, and my apartment is silent again. It feels better than before, being alone. The pine needles on the tree are still fresh, still beautiful, and I know it's not coming down any time soon.

Heading for Outers Retirement home, I pack up some extra cookies to take to my oldies. When I get there, everyone's still carrying on as before. Eddie is whispering sweet nothings into Ms. Peterson's ear. It still smells like candy and liniment, and all is well in the world.

Eddie turns around in his wheelchair and thrusts up his arms. "Jules! Where have you been all our lives! Get over here, weirdo!"

I grin. It's always nice to be called a weirdo by Eddie. What an old butthead he is. Oh how I missed him. Bending down I give him a hug, and he squeezes me tight. Ms.

Peterson moves to take out her hearing aids, and I laugh. "Don't worry, Ms. Peterson. No more complaining and whining from me."

"Oh? So you're engaged! Let me see the ring!" Ms. Peterson smiles, reaching for my hand.

"Well, no, I'm not. But I am all right with being single."

Eddie cocks an eyebrow and snickers. "What the hell happened to you in Wisconsin?"

A boy. A boy happened to me. Leaning in toward the two, I narrow my eyes. "I woke up this morning in my bed alone and I was fine. It felt great to be fine."

"I don't believe it. Who are you ringing in the New Year with? Who's your current fling of the month?" Eddie laughs, poking me in the arm.

"My television, Chinese food, and black and white movies. I don't need a guy to be comfortable with myself."

Ms. Peterson huffs and puffs, "Yeah right! You're engaged!" She scoops up my hand, showcasing the ring Kayden gave me and I laugh at her confusion.

"No, that's just—"

"My late wife's ring!" Eddie screams, looking at the ring. "You're wearing my Eloise's ring!"

Ms. Peterson's mouth drops and her hands move to her ears, taking out her hearing aids before she says, "Awkward…"

I chuckle at Eddie and roll my eyes, "No, it probably just looks like the same style."

Eddie reaches across the table and pulls the ring off my finger. "Yeah it just looks like it says E and E on the inside, huh? Where the hell did you get this? My grandson had it and he would never give this to anyone, unless…" A sudden realization hits Eddie while he looks up to meet my eyes. The palm of his hand slams down on the table, shaking Ms. Peterson's checkers pieces. "Well I'll be damned. Kayden's in love again."

My face heats up and my hands grow sweatier with every passing second. "What? No. Kayden isn't your…Kayden is your grandson?! No, that's not right." My chair slides across the carpeted floor and I stand. "I have to go."

"Sunshine," Eddie cries, and my heart stops beating. He wheels in his chair over to me; and, with shaking hands, he takes my hand in his and slips the ring back onto my finger. Then he pats my hand in his. "Kayden doesn't fall in love. He chooses to love."

"No, that's silly. We've only known each other for a few days. It was all an act, anyway. I hired—"

"Whoa, whoa, whoa. I didn't ask for your life story, kid. Look, go down to Hank's bar tonight, have a drink or five, and then ask Kayden to love you forever. It's that easy! I don't see why the kids of your generation complicate things so damn much. Put on a pretty dress, get some lipstick, and then go after my grandson. Just be warned though…he's an actor. So you'll probably be paying all of his bills for the rest of your life."

I grin at the happy old man and kiss his cheek, "Happy New Year, Eddie."

And I take off running to find a freaking dress.

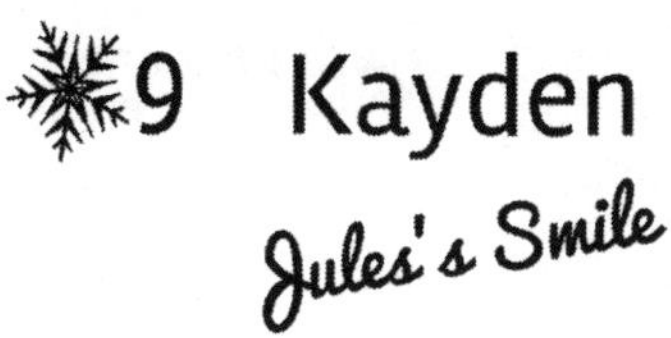

# 9 Kayden

## Jules's Smile

"Kayden, there is no reason for you to stay by my side every single day," Mom complains, pushing herself up from the living room couch, "There's no reason for anyone to keep babying me. I'm all right."

Aunt Sally is in the kitchen, cooking up some dinner for Mom and Dad, while Landon sits at the dining room table with his open laptop. I hate the ass, but the fact that he took the time away from the office to look after Mom says a lot. Kate has been stopping by whenever she's not working at the hospital, and Dad hasn't seen his office since Mom had the fall.

Gliding into the kitchen, I grab a dinner roll from the table. "Sticking around for the dinner?" Sally asks, checking the roast in the oven.

"Can't. It's New Year's Eve. The bar is gonna be crazy."

She huffs, tasting her gravy with her pinky finger. "Can I ask you something?"

"Shoot."

Her body swerves around toward me and she wipes her messy fingers on a paper towel. “Who’s the girl?”

I laugh, shaking my head back and forth. “I don’t know what you’re talking about.” Except I do. I know exactly what she’s talking about. She’s talking about me walking around for days humming Hall and Oates. She’s talking about me starting to open my mouth to tell her about Jules but shutting up just as quickly. She’s talking about the patch on my left arm and the lack of cigarettes resting between my lips.

“Yeah.” She walks over to me and flicks the patch on my arm. “Keep telling yourself that, kiddo. Whatever makes you sleep better at night.” Landon walks into the kitchen and grabs one of the dinner rolls, making Sally throw a fit. “Hell, boys, why don’t you eat the whole dinner while you’re at it? Why wait until we are sitting down for a damn meal?” She and her sassy attitude storm out of the room to check on Mom.

I lean against the counter, watching Landon pretend I’m invisible.

“I picked you for Secret Santa, Land,” I say, not quite sure where the words are coming from, or why I’m even saying them. He looks up to me, a sneer of annoyance stuck on his face. I keep talking, not really caring if he chooses to listen. “I didn’t get you anything because, well, I know nothing about you. So I thought as your gift I would tell you about me. When Penny died, a part of me left with her, but I didn’t lose my mind.

“What Jasmine told you I did, no matter how convincing she was, is a lie. There are rules to being a family, and I would never cross that line. I never told you that because I was so fucking pissed at you for not trusting me. Yeah, I screw up. I have sex with girls whose names I never ask for, and I let people down. But you’re my brother. You’re supposed to know me better than anyone. So for the record, I’m telling you that nothing fucking happened.” Tossing my hands up, I let out a short sigh, “There ya go. My secret Santa gift to you.”

Turning to walk away, I pause when I hear him respond to me.

“I broke up with her.” He runs his hands through his hair, picking his words carefully. “I’m sorry. I know it seems a little too late to say it but I am. I’m sorry. I’ve been an ass all this time and you didn’t deserve it. Sally’s right, isn’t she? There’s a girl?”

I twist around to look at him. “There’s a girl.”

He shifts his feet on the ground before crossing his arms and walking toward me. “Don’t fuck it up.”

I laugh, because it's too late. "Already did."

"I don't know." His head shakes and he starts moving past me into the next room, "If you're still alive, still breathing, I think it's never too late to try to make things better."

And he's out of my sight before I can reply. Mom walks over to me and places her hands against her hips. "Were you two just in the same room without screaming?"

I nod once, surprised like her. Kissing her forehead, I throw my jacket on to leave. "I have to get to work for the New Year's party. I'll be back tomorrow though."

Mom pulls me into her arms, holding me close. "If I had known you would stop by so much after I fell, I would have taken the tumble years ago." When we separate from our embrace, Dad's standing in the doorway, looking my way.

"Kayden," he hollers, a cigar hanging from his lips.

I don't have the strength in me to fight with him anymore. I don't have the power to listen to him tell me what a fuck up I am. There are so many things in my life I've wasted my time holding on to, wasted my time engaging. I don't want to do that anymore. I don't want to waste this one shot I have at life.

"Listen, Dad. I'm not a lawyer. I'm not. I'll never be a doctor. There's a good chance I will screw up again and again while I try to figure out what I want, who I am. But I can't handle you telling me, reinforcing the fact that I'm a loser. I'm getting another apartment you won't have to help pay for. I'm looking for a steadier job. I'm working on it, all right?"

His brows lower and he brushes his fingers across them, appearing to be deep in thought. When his head rises to meet my eyes, he sighs. "I was going to say thank you for being there for your mom."

Mom's eyes fill with tears, and I nudge her in the shoulder. "Always."

Dad's look of emotion doesn't last long, which is fine. He's not really that type of person. I get it. Before he turns to leave, he says, "Next Sunday dinner is at six. Bring a Mexican dish to pass."

I know it doesn't seem like much, and it hardly counts as an Oscar-winning performance, but Dad's short speech to me was pretty damn good. The fact that we just spoke without screaming at one another is a huge improvement from what we used to do.

Maybe, just maybe, I don't *fucking* hate him anymore.

Maybe I simply hate him.

Now *that's* progress.

The bar is packed by eleven, and I haven't stopped mixing drinks, getting hit on, and cleaning up shattered glass. There's a line of people wrapped around the building waiting to get inside, but I doubt anyone else is leaving this close to midnight. "What can I get you?" I ask a brunette who, in the past, I would've taken home for the night, but today all I want to do is mix her a damn drink before moving on to the next person.

"What do you suggest?" she flirts, barely wearing enough clothes to leave anything to the imagination. She's twirling her hair around her pinky, and it takes everything in my power to not roll my eyes at the girl.

"Oh my gosh, I hope I've never sounded that needy and desperate." The voice wakes me up as my eyes shift to the end of the bar. Somehow she possesses the power to put the world on pause. Jules smiles wide and her dimples kiss me from a distance. Her crazy, wild hair is tamed, but the curls bounce as they always do. She's wearing a beautiful red dress that covers everything while highlighting her curves. And her eyes…Jesus. I didn't know it was possible to miss a pair of eyes so much. I swear they're bluer or they sparkle more. Or well, maybe she's just happier. She looks happier.

I start to move her way, but she shakes her head, and points to the girl, waiting for her drink. Reaching under the counter, I open a random beer and slam it down. "Here you go. It's on the house."

"But…" the girl starts to whine while I'm already crossing to the other side of the bar.

"Hey, you," Jules screams over the loud music. The way she says those two simple words makes the world that much sweeter.

"What are you doing here?"

"I need to hire a fake boyfriend for New Year's Eve. You see, I was planning on spending my New Year's alone, drinking wine, and listening to Hall and Oates, but…I don't know. I'm feeling a little wild." She stands up straight and holds her hand out to me. "Help me up on the counter and then shut off the music."

I abide. Of course I fucking abide. She could have told me to jump in Lake Michigan and I would have performed the task butt-ass naked. The crowd goes nuts with the lost sound, but I don't care, Hank can fire me if he wants. *Please don't fire me, Hank.*

When she gets up there, she bends down to me, edging her lips close to mine. "By the way you look really sexdorable serving those drinks to people. Very sexdorable." She stretches back up to a standing position and she taps her hand right below her throat before speaking. "Hi! I'm Jules Stone. I'm single and weird, and I ugly cry—like real ugly. Snot, boogers, and all that gross stuff. I sometimes snort when I laugh too hard, and I am desperately in need of a date for New Year's Eve. I need a kiss in about thirty minutes. I'm offering fifty dollars to whoever will step up to the job. So if anyone's interested—"

"I'll do it!" A stranger yells in the background. Followed by more and more people shouting. Jules' face expression changes, and I can tell, like always, she didn't really think her plan through.

"Hell," The brunette I slid a beer to steps onto the bar and walks over to Jules. "I'll do it!" She wraps Jules in her arms, dips her, and kisses her—hard.

The crowd goes wild. Jules's doe eyes are untamed and confused, and Hank turns the music back on. My gut hurts from laughing so hard at the shocked look frozen on Sunshine's face. "Jules, get down."

I take her hand in mine and help her get down behind the counter so she's standing in front of me. "I just kissed a girl, and her tongue touched my tongue I think… And her hand grabbed my ass. That definitely didn't go the way I thought it would. In the movies, there's always this big moment of realization where the hero or heroine marches into a place, confesses his or her love in a big life-changing way, and it works out perfectly."

I blink once, looking down to the ground, and a realization hits me when my head snaps back up, my eyes widen. "Did you say 'confesses love'?"

"Lust." She pauses, wiggling her nose and slapping her hand across her face. "*Lust*. I meant lust. I mean, clearly we don't love each other yet. I've known you for like, a week. And there were at least five days where we didn't even communicate. I tagged those as the lost days. So love is a little extreme and—"

She's rambling, I love it. My finger moves to her lips and shuts them. "I'm sorry I lied about the agency. I was trying to prove people wrong, prove myself to myself, I guess. And if I have to, I will spend the rest of my days trying to make it up to you. Because I lust you, too."

"Do you really? I mean, I know I'm odd and stuff. My family almost drove you crazy, too, and I really messed up this romantic, big life-changing moment. If you give me another day, I can come up with something even cooler, something more fun! I'm thinking clowns and a marching band."

"Jules, shut up. This isn't a movie." I inch my lips closer to hers and ignore all of the people begging for drinks. Our lips are touching, but we're not kissing—yet. "This is real life."

"Real? No more fake?"

"No more fake."

"Like a totally, ridiculously, *real* relationship?" Her smile widens and I want nothing more than to fall for her for the remainder of my life.

"Kiss me now."

She shrugs her shoulders and flips her hair over her shoulder. "My breath smells like tequila and the Chinese food I decided to eat before I came. We can't kiss right now. I want the first real kiss to be gentle. Calm and perfectly sweet. Romantic, peppermint-scented, soft, and no tongue of course because that would just be tacky. Plus, we're in a bar. Gross, right? I hate bars. I think I want the first kiss to—"

It doesn't matter what she wants. When my lips lock with hers, I feel her body melt against mine. She kisses back like she means it, and I lose myself in the moment. I kiss her deeper because I've been waiting years to find *this* girl, *this* kiss, *this* feeling. *This* moment, *this* connection, *this* experience… Jules Stone doesn't simply feel like home—she is home. Our eyes open, and we remain still, not pulling away from one another. I never want to pull away from the light before me.

When our lips separate, I step back and take in all of her beauty. "I have to finish up work, but at midnight, I'm going to kiss you again, and again, and again. Then, after everyone clears out and it's almost three in the morning, I'm going to turn on your favorite song, and we are going to dance until sunrise." I say. She smiles, and it's evident I'm the luckiest man in the world to be speaking to her.

"And then you'll make me pancakes?" Her voice sings and those damn dimples almost knock me over in a wave of ecstasy as I kiss the palm of her hand.

And then I'll make her pancakes.

She's beautiful, my Sunshine, and I hope her glow always lights my way.

# 10 Jules

## This Christmas

**-One Year Later-**

"Okay. Just remember, don't be yourselves. Be anything but yourselves." I stand on the porch of Kayden's parents' home, pointing a finger at all of my family members. It's been a year since Kayden's and my made-up relationship launched, and for some reason, he thought it would be a fun idea for our families to meet during the holiday.

I'm pretty sure he was wasted when he came up with the idea.

His grandmother's engagement ring is still resting on my finger, and in a month, we will be standing in front of all of our loved ones, saying, 'I do.' But first I just want to make it through Christmas dinner.

"Grandma! Is that a flask?! Stop drinking!" I whine, grabbing the bottle from her hands. *Jesus*! "Everyone, act like an every day, All-American family. Okay?"

"Julie Anne, stop it! We are perfectly capable of being entertainingly witty, and down to earth in front of your boyfriend's family!" Mom hisses, flipping her hair over her shoulder. Her four thousand dollar earrings say differently. Down to earth people don't wear four thousand dollar earrings!

"Jules, your mother's right. Don't worry. We're actors! This is what we do!" Dad insists, knocking on the front door. My nerves must be all over the place, because when he knocks, it feels like he's punching me in my gut.

Lisa is standing next to Olivia, with no Danny in sight. She says he has to work, but doesn't go into more detail about it, probably because I really don't care where he is. "So this family…they really believe in the Christmas decorations thing, huh?" she asks, looking around at the decked out yard, with a singing Santa and a six-foot tall snowman planted in the middle of the lawn.

The front door opens and I can't help but smile when I see Kayden on the other side. "Hey, babe." He pulls me close and kisses the top of my head. "Hey everyone! So happy you're here."

Dad walks over and gently smacks Kayden in the arm. "Rumor has it you signed with Simon and Simons Talent Agency in L.A.! That's brilliant!" Kayden's smile shows his personal pride and nods as my Dad wraps him in a celebratory hug.

"Yeah, it's been a good week. Jules's television pilot premiere is in a few weeks, too. We went to the screening of the first three episodes last weekend. She's amazing in it." Kayden is bragging about me and I want to hit him for making me feel so uncomfortable.

"It's a winter premiere. I'm a side character. The show's not primetime television, and we aren't even sure if it will be picked up for the full season. It's not that amazing," I say, trying to downplay my excitement over my first ever television role.

Kayden lowers his brows and those green eyes of his lock with my blues. "It's nothing less than outstanding." He still makes my cheeks redden, the way he believes in me, the way he supports me no matter what. It's not long before Kayden's dad is standing in the front foyer, ready to welcome my family into his home.

"Hi everyone. I'm Steve, welcome! We're glad you're here."

Dad is the first to hold out his hand, "Hi, I'm Matt Stone, and this is my family. Yes, we are famous and yes, we have millions and millions of dollars. But, don't let those small facts make you think we aren't just your every day normal family. The only difference is that we poop gold."

"And drink like fish." Grandma chimes in, and I giggle watching Mom roll her eyes.

"*Mom*! Fish don't drink! What a silly comment," my mom hisses to Grandma.

"And how do you know that? How do you know fish don't drink? Did you study fish at some damn point of your life? Do you have a degree in fish lifestyles?" Grandma hollers while pushing her way into the house. "Kayden, where's the bar?"

"Straight back, to your left." Kayden gestures into the house. Dad and Steve march off with Grandma, to each grab a drink, and cigar, of their own.

We all enter the house, and the feeling of pressure is still mocking me. Mom looks toward the kitchen, where Kayden's mother Heather and his Aunt Sally are cooking. "I'm going to go introduce myself and set down this beautiful cake I made."

"Mom." I arch an eyebrow and watch as she rolls her eyes at me.

"Okay, the cake that my chef made. Really, Jules. Do you have to be such a freak about the details?"

Out of nowhere, two teenage boys come running through the living room, screaming about video games or something. Sally pokes her head out of the kitchen and hollers toward them. “Boys! I swear if you two wake up your baby brother I will make your lives a living hell! Video games! Upstairs! *Now*!” Sally runs her hands over her apron, and the smile on her face expands when she looks up to me. “Hey, Jules! Merry Christmas!” She’s quick to move over toward us and introduces herself to Lisa and Olivia.

“It’s nice to meet you, Sally. Whatever you ladies are cooking up in the kitchen smells heavenly.” Lisa grins and is the perfect amount of charming.

“Yeah, that’s no thanks to me. Heather only lets me cut the vegetables. So if you come across a huge chuck of celery in your stuffing—you’re welcome.” Sally winks, and bends down low to look at Olivia. “My daughter Hailey is in the back room watching all of her favorite Disney movies. Do you want to join her?”

Before I can blink, Olivia runs off to the back room.

“So, you’re the girl dating that Danny Everson guy?” Sally asks, and Lisa nods once in reply. “He always seemed like an ass to me.”

“He is,” Both Lisa and I say at the same time.

"Sorry," I apologize for calling the father of her kid an asshole. But if the shoe fits…

"We broke up." Lisa confesses in such a nonchalant manner, I almost wonder if she's serious. "It turns out he found a new co-star to get to know." She smiles, but I see the tears she's trying to hold back. I don't know what to say, because I know how she feels. Crushed. Moving to her, I pull her into a hug, mouthing an apology.

"Everything okay in here?" At the sound of a deep voice, Lisa and I separate in time to see Landon entering the room. Lisa stands tall and shoots Landon her killer 'I think you're hot' smile. Landon smirks when he sees her looking his way. "Is Lisa Stone standing in front of me?"

She holds her hand out toward him, and he's quick to kiss her palm. Well, if she's going to hit on a Reece, I'm just happy it's not Kayden.

"My gawd, Ms. Hollywood. You sure are fast to get over your ex-boyfriend. Come on, to the kitchen to help cook." Sally wraps my sister's arm around hers and pulls her away after Lisa flashes Landon one last grin.

"Maybe I can help?" Landon offers, chasing the two toward the kitchen.

It's not long before we hear a screaming baby through the walkie-talkie sitting on the coffee table, and Sally steps in our direction to attend to her now four month-old baby boy.

"Don't worry, Sally. We'll check on him." Kayden takes my hand and leads me to the back bedroom. Baby Cole is crying his eyes out, and I lift him from his crib, snuggling his body against mine.

"He's so little," I whisper, rocking him back and forth. Kayden grins without replying and slides his hands into his jeans pockets. Cringing from the sound of falling pots, I glance out the bedroom door. "It's going well, right? I mean, Grandma's drunk. Dad's smoking a cigar with Steve already. That's good, right?" I run my fingers through my hair, muttering my thoughts out loud. "Lisa and Mom could be pretty dangerous in the kitchen. Let's just say they aren't the best around that area. And…"

"You're rambling. Everyone's going to have a wonderful time. And if not, well…I hid a bottle of whiskey under the bathroom cupboard." Kayden walks over to me and rubs his hands up and down my shoulders. I can't help but relax when I feel his touch. Baby Cole is relaxing, too, falling back to sleep in my arms.

"Oh," I shake my head back and forth, and lay Cole back into his crib. "I can't drink." Reaching into my back pocket, I pull out a pregnancy test and watch Kayden's eyes widen in shock as he grabs the test from my hands.

"You were carrying a pee stick in your back pocket this whole time?" He questions, smiling at the positive sign on the stick.

"Yeah…is that weird and gross?"

"Sooo weird and gross. So, you're pregnant? Right now? We're pregnant?"

"Sooo pregnant." I smirk as he places the pregnancy test down. Then he wraps an arm around my lower back, pulling me closer to him. Baby Cole starts crying again, but to tell you the truth it's the perfect backdrop noise for this moment in time. It's a beautiful, life-changing sound that's a welcomed gift to our lives.

"Well, look what we have here." Kayden points above us to the invisible mistletoe. Our lips have not yet touched, but our hearts are already so deeply entwined. "I love you, my Sunshine."

"I love you, too."

He lips brush against mine, and I am absolutely crazy about the simplicity of the kiss. It's perfect, it's real, and it's ours.

It's almost ridiculous how real we are, but I'm totally okay with that.

34376403R00139

Made in the USA
San Bernardino, CA
02 May 2019